“It *has* .
Because honestly, I really don’t want you living rent free in my head when some other guy is trying to get into my pants.”

“*What other guy, Violet?*”

“That’s not the point, Torres,” she said, frowning as she looked up at him. The fading light caused dramatic shadows beneath his brow and cheekbones.

“I can assure you it’s *entirely* the point.”

She threw her hands up in exasperation, but he was so close her fingertips brushed briefly against his chest. She swallowed a gasp at the intensity of her body’s response from that simple, accidental touch. “You do not get to go all caveman, Torres. You don’t get to give a shit about men who *actually* want me, when you don’t.”

THE PROTECTOR'S VOW

SHADOW TEAM SIX BOOK TWO

LEAH ASHTON

Copyright © 2022 by Leah Ashton

All rights reserved.

No part of this book may be reproduced in any form or by any electronic or mechanical means, including information storage and retrieval systems, without written permission from the author, except for the use of brief quotations in a book review.

This is a work of fiction. Characters, places and incidents are either the product of the author's imagination or are used fictitiously. Any resemblance to actual persons (living or dead) is entirely coincidental.

ISBN 978-0-6488598-9-5

First print edition published September 2022

PROLOGUE

The Grande Fox & Laughton Hotel

An undisclosed location in the Middle East

Five years ago

The only person in the world who called Andy, *Andrew*, was Andy Torres' fiancée, Natalie.

Andy leaned back in his white wicker chair to read her latest text.

Good morning Andrew! (that's right, isn't it? I'm so bad at time zone math!) xxoo

She'd attached a selfie of her wearing one of his old T-shirts in their bed as she blew him a kiss.

He replied as the other men at the restaurant table chatted around him. Across from him was Tyler Cerra – or Cez – fellow Delta Force Operator, while the other three men he barely knew. Two were Navy SEALs and the other a Marine Raider, all also on Rest & Relaxation thanks to a new agreement between this fancy luxury hotel and the United States Armed Forces. It was day three of R&R for him and Cez after completing a tense, complex prisoner exchange mission in Afghanistan. The Navy SEALs – Devin and Garrett – had arrived a few days before, and after Devin invited them to share their table the first morning, this opulent buffet breakfast had become their morning routine. Cez and the other dude at the table – Caleb, the Marine Raider – had also been hitting the local bars each evening. Both apparently had a successful night out – Andy absolutely knew for sure that Cez had, given he'd met the pretty British backpacker he'd brought home when she'd crept out of Cez's room – as well as heard them both through the surprisingly thin walls of their two-bedroom suite at about 3am. And the way Caleb's gaze was tracking a woman in a tight white dress as she navigated the busy buffet tables with a knowing swing to her hips suggested he was keen to continue that acquaintance.

Morning sweet cheeks, Andy replied to Nat. *Miss you.*

And he did. He hadn't been home in nearly a year, which was far too long. The entirety of his relationship with Nat had been like this though – moments captured between deployments. He was damn lucky she put up with him.

Dev was waving some tall guy over to their table who Andy didn't know, but he was definitely military. Dev seemed to be collecting every stray soldier he could find at this place. Didn't bother Andy, but equally he would've been totally fine just hanging out with Cez for the week. He and Cez had been tight for years, ever since Delta Force selection almost five years ago now. They'd been in the same operational squadron ever since, and despite the stark difference in their sex lives – Cez with his movie-star Italian good looks couldn't seem to exist without women hitting on him, while Andy was happily the always-partnered guy – they just got each other. There was an ease to the shit they talked that'd got them both through some dark moments in their Delta Force careers. You saw shit and *did* shit in this job that meant you needed good people around you. And that's what Tyler Cerra was – good people. There was no one in the world Andy trusted more than Cez.

Devin introduced the stranger to the table. His name was Sam Taberner, and he was Special Forces, just like the rest of them.

"Call me Cez," Tyler said to Sam, after introducing himself.

"Maybe not as loudly as that girl last night, hey?" Andy quipped, not about to let a chance to let an easy swing at Cez go to the catcher. "Need my beauty sleep, my man, and she was like a damn foghorn: *Cheeezzzzz,*" he groaned loudly, attracted the attention of the neighboring tables. Cez threw his linen napkin and Andy let it hit him in the forehead.

"Fuck off," Cez said good naturedly. He turned back to Sam and shrugged. "Not gonna apologize for making a lady feel good. Andy here just needs to stop pressing his ear up against my bedroom door." He dropped his voice to a mock whisper. "We all know that's as close as he's getting to any action."

Cez did have a point there. Andy had never – and would never – cheat. His dead-beat asshole of a father had fucked around on his mom whenever he hadn't been smacking her around, so he had no doubts about the kind of man he was determined to be. But his seeming inability to remain single meant each deployment was always a desert of a dry spell. Did make coming home pretty amazing though. Welcome home sex was damn miraculous.

He threw the napkin back with interest, although Cez caught it mid-air.

"*Seu cu de burro,*" Andy said. "And a total slut."

"And proud of it," Cez replied. "Maybe not the first part though. What's a burro? A horse?"

"You're a donkey's ass," Andy translated. His mom's Brazilian family had taught him a broad selection of Portuguese profanities. "Obviously."

Cez looked thoughtful. "Nope," he said, after a moment. "I'm a fucking work of art."

The banter continued as Andy introduced himself to Sam, before the conversation moved onto Caleb.

Andy lifted his phone to take a photo of the restaurant to send to Nat. It had to be said, this hotel was by far the nicest place he'd ever stayed. It was brand new, but a tribute to classic Middle Eastern architecture, with lots of tall marble pillars and double height arched windows. Beyond the open windows kids shrieked happily as they played in the lagoon-like pool beneath the already hot morning sun. There was a whole chain of Fox & Laughton's across the world, and while he wasn't interested in being this close to his work on his honeymoon, maybe one of the Fox & Laughton's in Europe would suit.

He snapped a photo and sent it to Nat. *Honeymoon inspo?*

Cez, of course, thought he was insane to want to get married at his age: *You're twenty-seven, man. What's the rush?* But Andy felt really good about it. Cez loved the thrill of the new and exciting, while Andy loved knowing he'd have Nat by his side for the rest of his life. There was a comfort to it, and while he didn't mind hearing about Cez's wild stories, he had no interest in emulating them.

He looked up from his phone as he clocked the tension around the table. It seemed Garrett –who'd said barely a word to anyone in the past two days – had an issue with Sam. Cez raised his eyebrows at Andy across the table and grinned, loving the drama.

"Garrett Walker," the massive, previously-silent guy grunted at Sam. "Navy SEAL, and former resident of Falcon, Colorado." He paused. "The dirt-poor part, which is why a Taberner would never have deigned to know my name."

"You're a Walker?" Sam asked, clearly stunned.

Andy knew nothing about Falcon, or Garrett's family heritage, but the animosity that rolled off the SEAL was palpable.

"That's what I said," Garrett grunted, then re-opened the book in his hand. The guy always had a book with him.

"I've read that," Sam said in an affable tone. "I like the next book in the series the best."

Garrett just kept on reading. "Your parents wouldn't want you talking to trash like me, *Sam*," he said, his eyes on the page.

Sam's affability went out the window. "*Fuck*, man. Want to shove that chip off your shoulder? Don't know what your beef is with me, but I am certain I was never in class with you, let alone took your place on the baseball team, or stole your girl or did anything I can think of to deserve this hostility." He pushed back his chair. "Thanks Devin, but I'll go wait for a table. I don't have time for this shit."

Dev shoved his own chair back and went to follow Sam.

Andy looked at Cez. "Man, that was randomly intense—"

But a shockingly loud noise silenced Andy's words in his throat.

An explosion. Nearby. Like *right next to this room.*

Smoke poured into the dining room as a split second of eerie silence transitioned into a cacophony of terrified screams.

As one, all six of the men stood.

Was it a bomb? A terrible accident?

It didn't matter. Surrounded by scores of petrified people and hotel staff with panicked-glazed expressions, the immediate priority was obvious.

"We need to get everyone out of here," Andy barked. "And check for casualties."

He met Cez's gaze and his teammate gave a sharp nod. "Cerra and I are trained medics," he said, "we'll go this way." He pointed where smoke still poured through the doorway.

"I'm a medic, too," Caleb said. "I'll go with you." The woman in the white dress stumbled as she ran towards him, grabbing his arm.

"No—" the woman gasped. "What if there are more bombs, Caleb?"

Dev cut her off. "Ma'am, we need to get everyone out of this building."

The sound of not too-distant gunfire resolved any lingering question of the cause of the explosion. But the sound had come from outside the hotel, not inside. They had a little time, maybe.

The room was beginning to move in an uncontrolled wave of panic.

"Torres, Cerra, Grey – you go." It was Garrett, his words clear and definite. "McCarthy... and Taberner, let's get these people to safety and work out what the fuck is going on."

What the fuck is *going on?*

At a run, Andy headed for the lobby to find out.

ONE

Cars & Coffee

Falcon, Colorado.

One year ago.

Violet Chapman took a long, deep breath before she opened her car door.

She sat in the parking lot of the business she remembered as Falcon Tire & Lube, but it had become Cars & Coffee sometime in the ten years since she'd last lived in the picturesque and gossipy town of Falcon, Colorado.

She had a job interview in exactly six minutes as office manager for this mash-up of an auto repair shop and café. She'd bumped into her one-time babysitter, Casey Taberner, at Walgreens two days earlier, and their brief conversation had led to this interview with Casey's brother. She didn't entirely get why Sam Taberner had decided that cars and coffee went together, but she wasn't complaining. Should she get this job, caffeine would definitely help soften this dramatic fall from grace.

Ha! Unlikely.

She was under no illusions she'd already hit rock bottom. Even easy-access to almond milk lattes wasn't going to change the reality that three months back she'd been fired from her dream job. Worse, she'd destroyed her professional reputation, with her blacklisting clear after dozens of applications for roles back in New York had failed to secure a single interview. Sure, the HR executives hadn't come out and said it, but despite recent appearances to the contrary, she wasn't an idiot. *So, what you're saying is you're not interested in interviewing me - the person you head-hunted not even six months ago - because my experience isn't a great fit for your organization?*

The answers to her progressively less tactful questions had always been a firm version of: *we're never going to hire you, please go away,* even though the exact words used were quite different.

Violet Chapman had fucked up spectacularly.

She'd been a senior data and analytics strategist for a huge pharmaceutical firm in New York, and being actively groomed for the role of executive vice president. She'd always loved numbers and data, and her drive and attention to detail had been her ticket out of Falcon. No one had ever expected Violet Chapman to go to college, but she'd made it happen and then worked her butt off to succeed in her data analytics career. But those student loans from her wonderful years at UChicago had now forced her back to Falcon, and to this parking lot at Cars & Coffee.

The loans that'd felt a small price to pay for her lucrative career now threatened to drown her. Once she'd had healthy savings, but they'd already dwindled down to near nothing. With no job and no prospects, she'd retreated to Falcon and her old bedroom in her 81-year-old Nanna's house. But like everyone in the Chapman family, her Nanna had no money. For years Violet had sent her a portion of her paycheck, but now she had no paycheck to share. She needed a job, and this one at least felt vaguely relevant to Violet's skillset. Heck, maybe an MBA was overkill for the Cars & Coffee office manager, but Violet wasn't too proud to work here. In fact, she was *desperate* to work here.

She needed an income, fast. Money first, and once she was back on her feet she'd work out if there was anything left to salvage of her career.

But after what she'd done, she doubted it.

She opened the door, and in her very best heels with her shoulders back, she strode from her car to the office.

The instant Andy saw her, he went still. He'd just handed a café mocha to the last of the group of moms who'd become Cars & Coffee regulars after school drop off. As the group of chatty women walked away with their collection of strollers and feisty toddlers, his gaze landed on the woman in the sharp charcoal skirt suit and lime green heels and he was... transfixed.

He just stood in the renovated 1960s teardrop caravan-come-coffee van, and stared.

She was tall, with long legs and curvy hips. Her hair was a dark red, styled in a sleek low bun, and her glasses were a bold emerald green. He wasn't close enough to be certain, but he just knew she had freckles dusted across her long, narrow nose. She appeared to have no awareness of his attention as she walked with purpose to the office.

She was here for an interview with Sam, he knew that. Sam's sister had recommended her, he thought – and he knew Sam already planned to hire her. *She's smart and needs a job,* he'd said. He also knew her name: Violet. It suited her, the vividness of her hair and heels reminding him of the vibrance of his mom's window-boxes full of violas in Philadelphia.

She paused at the office door, and he watched her shoulders lift and drop as she took several deep breaths. Nothing about her appearance fitted in with her surroundings. She looked like she'd made a wrong turn on her way to a boardroom in LA or New York City. She looked perfect and very, very expensive.

She took another deep breath, then glanced over her shoulder. He didn't move and she mustn't have seen him in the shadows of the van, while the rest of the lot was empty. Caleb was working on an SUV on a lift beyond the open roller-doors of the garage, but his back was to the woman.

As Andy watched, she quickly slid one hand down

her butt, pinched at the snug fabric of her skirt, and wiggled her hips.

He swallowed a laugh as she adjusted her underwear. This perfect, elegant, beautiful woman had a wedgie. It was so god-damn adorable it finally snapped him out of his almost trance.

Or maybe that was just because now he was trying to imagine the type of panties she wore.

She knocked on the office door, and he took a step back from the coffee van's open window.

What the fuck was he doing? He gripped the countertop and shook his head.

This wasn't like him. Twelve months since he'd moved to Falcon, and he'd never been tempted to break one extremely simple rule: No dating local women.

And you didn't get much more local than a woman you might be working with.

He had another rule too: No complications.

He'd learned a lot in the four years since that ill-fated breakfast at the Fox & Laughton. He'd learned even more in the two years since he'd joined the Shadow Team. And one of those lessons was that Andy Torres was way too good at complications. His life of serial monogamy had meant the entirety of his adulthood had been intertwined with his girlfriend of the moment. He'd been all tangled up all the time and hadn't even realized it. In fact, he'd reveled in those ties and knots, loving how they'd pulled him tight, thinking that was what life was, thinking that was what he'd wanted. But once he'd understood that those promises and expectations were as substantial and enduring as a spider's web, he'd begun to see life differently. To see it as it *really* is.

To see *himself* as he really was.

And that man he now realized he was? That guy at the Fox & Laughton wouldn't even recognize him. He wouldn't even *like* him. He'd been changed forever that day, even if it had taken another two years for him to comprehend it.

The woman with the freckles and the sexy-as-hell walk wasn't for him.

He had absolutely no business gawking at her.

Even if she was interested, he had nothing to offer her. He had nothing to offer any woman other than an uncomplicated fuck.

And *that* woman, she was complicated. He was as confident of that as he was in his right hook in the boxing ring. Which was to say: he'd stake his life on it.

A car drove into the parking lot, and a little further along the sidewalk another daily regular – a greyhound named Stewart and his podiatrist owner – were also approaching.

He ran a hand through his hair as he glanced over at the office. Through the blinds he could just make out the woman's shape in the chair across from Sam's desk.

He rapped his fist not-too-gently against his forehead.

Not for you, man.

If she got the job, he was keeping his distance.

TWO

"You've got the job," Sam said.

"Pardon me?"

Violet had literally just sat down. The office was clean but chaotic, the single desk filled with multiple in-trays piled with miscellaneous papers and an elderly desktop computer with a screen that might've been considered a reasonable size in 2002.

"Would you like a coffee while we discuss the role?" Sam asked. He sat behind the desk, but looked awkward. He wasn't really an office kinda guy. She didn't know him that well, and only through his sister, Casey, who had babysat her many, many years ago. But even so, she knew of his long military career, although even if she hadn't, she would've picked it. He was still super fit; with the black Cars & Coffee t-shirt he wore clearly showing off his many muscles. He was four years older than her twenty-nine years, but she'd known he'd been a bit of a heart-throb at Falcon High. Personally, she didn't really get it. Maybe it was because she remembered him as a teenage boy? She found him handsome in almost an abstract way. Like, it was a fact, but it didn't impact *her* in anyway.

Which she guessed was a good thing for the work environment.

Especially given her very recent... professional misstep.

She shook her head at the unwanted memory. She was here to get a new job, not obsess over the one she'd lost.

Although apparently... she already *had* this job?

"No coffee?" Sam prompted.

"Oh," she said, gathering her thoughts. "No, thank you. Sorry – don't you need to interview me first?"

He shrugged. "Why? You're insanely overqualified and Casey's vouched for you. That's enough for me."

She frowned. "You don't want to ask me *why* I've applied for this job?"

"Do you want to tell me?"

She sat back in her chair. "Not particularly. I just need it."

He gave a sharp nod. "That's enough for me. Figure you have a reason for returning to Falcon, just like I did."

"And you don't talk about your reason?" she guessed.

"Got it in one," he said. Then grinned. "So, should we discuss this role I'm certain you could do standing on your head?"

For the first time in months she felt the tension in her

neck and shoulders ease, just slightly. "Yes, please," she said.

HALF AN HOUR later Sam gave her a tour of the garage. She met the two mechanics working away inside – a tall, gruff man called Dev, and a younger, lankier, friendlier guy called Caleb. Both were as fit as Sam, which while Casey had explained how Sam had re-opened his dad's old business with a group of fellow military veterans, was still rather surprising. All three men were just so big and muscular, as if they were ready to be deployed again tomorrow. Clearly none of them had let themselves go in retirement.

Sam's cell phone rang as they headed over to the coffee van to meet the last of the Cars & Coffee employees. He apologized as he indicated he needed to take the call, before walking briskly to the office, leaving Violet alone.

Sam had told her it was Andy who really ran the coffee side of his business. Andy had joined Cars & Coffee last, and had taken over from a muddled roster of each mechanic working in the van. *I just wanted a coffee van;* Sam had explained with a shrug. *Didn't really put enough thought into how to run the thing.*

Already Violet had learned that was Sam's approach to his entire business. When she'd asked him about his scheduling system, or book-keeping – even how he accepted payment from clients – he'd just shrug again.

What we're good at is fixing cars, he'd said. *The rest is what we need you for.*

The one thing Sam did have in hand was the work roster. This, he'd explained, he ran himself, and would continue to do so. His tone had become serious as he'd explained that a work-life balance was important to him, and because their military experiences impacted the Cars & Coffee team in different ways, the roster was flexible and changeable.

In contrast to the haphazard office, the coffee van was beautifully neat and tidy. The retro teardrop shape was painted the same dramatic dark blue-grey as the garage, and every piece of chrome gleamed in the morning sun. The long window down the side of the van was propped open, revealing a mostly white interior with an expensive looking coffee machine, and an oak counter that jutted out from the window. A chalkboard attached to the side neatly listed the menu beneath the Cars & Coffee logo with its 1960s font.

Violet waited as the man inside served a couple. His back was to her as he frothed milk at the espresso machine. It appeared every man who worked here had enormous shoulders. It was almost comical how large the man looked in the cute little van.

"Violet Chapman? Is that you?"

It was the woman waiting for her coffee. She had silver hair, long and straight to her shoulders.

Violet blinked as she recognized her. "Ms Sheffield?"

The woman laid her hand on the arm of the man beside her. "*Mrs* Smythe-Sheffield now," she corrected.

"Or rather, Harriet, I suppose. I'm not your English teacher anymore."

Her words were friendly, but Violet crossed her arms. "No," she agreed.

"Well!" Harriet said, her gaze sweeping up and down Violet's body. "I'd heard you'd returned to Falcon. All the way from *New York!*" As her husband turned and handed Harriet her coffee, she smiled up at him. "You know," she said, as if Violet wasn't there. "Violet here *shocked* the town with her success. Who would've thought it! Your Nanna is so proud, she keeps all of Falcon updated." She turned back to Violet. "I always knew you had it in you," she said.

You never showed it, Violet thought – but remained silent. Her English teacher had not been alone in her low expectations of her.

"So, what brings you back to Falcon?" Harriet asked.

Violet pasted on a big smile. "Oh, I just couldn't knock back the opportunity to work at Cars & Coffee," she said brightly.

Harriet raised her eyebrows. "But your mom told Luanne – who works at the diner, you know? – that your fancy job paid so much you were richer than Croesus."

This was not the first time in her life her mom's loose tongue and accompanying embellishments were utterly unhelpful.

Harriet's gaze grew speculative. "Young Sam is doing quite well with his dad's old business, but he's not offering a New York salary. Please don't say your dear Nanna is unwell?"

Violet swallowed a sigh. Honestly, how was this the business of an old high school teacher she hadn't even liked? And who hadn't liked her? "My Nanna will outlive us all," she said firmly. "Now, I'm sure your coffees are getting cold—"

"Did something happen in New York? I heard a dreadful rumor..."

Ah, she'd been silly to assume any of this conversation was innocent. Had Harriet-Ms Sheffield-Mrs Smythe-Whatsit only come to Cars & Coffee to sniff out gossip?

It wasn't even a question.

"...at the 2Ps Salon that there was some scandal in New York. Of course, *I* said that rumor couldn't be true." She gave a shrill laugh. "We all know it's your *mother* that's the truly scandalous Chapman in Falcon, not you, Violet."

The pause that followed could only be described as anticipatory.

Oh, for fuck's sake.

Violet gritted her teeth as fury made her blood run hot.

Her whole damn life she'd dealt with this crap. Her Nanna had brought her up, but her mom never left Falcon, so her mom's mistakes and reputation just added to the pain of having a mother who lived on the other side of town but barely bothered to see her. The residents of Falcon had always assumed her mother's history of bad taste in (many) men and terrible decisions with drugs would – for sure – be inherited by her daughter. This meant she'd grown up constantly having to prove herself. And often the need to do so had made her so angry she hadn't even bothered. *You think I'm a petty thief like my mom?* Fine, I'll steal the bitchy head cheerleader's new lipstick, then. *You think I'm a slut?* Fine, I'll never deny any salacious rumor, even though none are true. *You think I'll never make anything of my life?* Fine, I'll half-ass my way through high school.

It was her Nanna who eventually dragged Violet out of her cycle of self-sabotage. At age sixteen Violet had finally comprehended her Nanna's grief as she helplessly observed the shambles of her only child's life, and her Nanna's horror as she thought her only grand-daughter was about to do the same.

Her guilt was what turned things around, although it was too late for anyone in Falcon to believe she'd changed... or realize she'd never really been the wayward girl she'd sometimes appeared to be.

And now *this* woman...*this* teacher who'd never bothered to see past the rumors and assumptions of her youth... she was smugly standing here, hoping for every detail of the downfall that would re-affirm what she wanted to believe: That Violet Chapman was just as messed up and as trashy as her mom.

When the tightness in her throat loosened enough to allow her to speak, her words shook with fury. "Who the fu—"

"Sam made an offer Violet couldn't refuse," a deep voice interrupted.

Violet's tirade lodged in her throat as she looked up

and into the coffee van – where the man with the huge shoulders currently leaned casually against the oak counter.

"Sam's a savvy guy," the man continued. "And he knows he needs the best when it comes to running his business. He treats his father's legacy with the respect it deserves." *Respect* had a hard edge, but the man's expression was affable. "And he *respects* Violet's business knowledge, and is thrilled she is willing to work with Cars & Coffee to optimize and expand his business." He gave a casual shrug. "So, it's just like Violet said. An opportunity she couldn't knock back."

She didn't know how he did it, but despite his relaxed posture and ever-present smile, the man was... intimidating. There was a hardness to his gaze – a deep hazel gaze that's brutality did not match his smile. A gaze that was downright hostile.

He looked at Violet, and when his gaze softened as it met hers, her stomach flipped over. Somehow she didn't hear what he said the first time, so he repeated himself.

"Anything else you'd like to add, Violet?" he asked.

She swallowed, all flustered. She dragged her attention back to Harriet, but now the woman just looked like an old, tired version of the teacher she'd never liked all that much – and not worth any of her time, or anger. She rolled her shoulders back.

"No," she said briskly. And left it at that.

"Oh," Harriet said. "I was just—"

"Leaving," the man finished for her, pushing up from the counter as his smile grew even broader.

Violet added, "before those coffees get cold!"

With an owlish blink, Violet's one-time English teacher nodded at the man, then at Violet, then walked briskly from the lot, her husband a step behind her, his gaze everywhere but on them.

Now it was Violet's turn to blink owlishly as her brain struggled to catch up with what had just happened.

The broad-shouldered man had disappeared from view, but then she heard a metallic slam before he materialized beside her in the shadow of the caravan's open window.

She had to tilt her chin upwards to look at him as he was as stupidly tall as the rest of the men who worked here. His skin was a golden tan and his dark brows contrasted with the arresting green edged-gold of his eyes. His hair was thick, dark and too long at the sides, and looked like he constantly ran his hands through it. He wore a Cars & Coffee T-Shirt, the exact same style as the other men she'd met – yet with him she *really* noticed the shape of his biceps, and where the soft fabric clung to the strength of his pectoral muscles.

She yanked her gaze upwards, taking in the shadow of attractive stubble and his even more attractive mouth. His nose wasn't quite straight, and the hard lines to his jaw and cheekbones meant he wasn't classically handsome, like Sam. But he was... gorgeous.

The force of her reaction to him shocked her. She stood, staring at him, her heart racing and her skin prickly with awareness as she felt her cheeks grow hot.

"I'm Violet Chapman," she said stupidly, given he'd already said her name and clearly knew who she was.

"Andy Torres," he said. "Barista and sometimes mechanic."

"And sometimes defender of strangers," she added.

He frowned. "I have no doubt your old teacher deserved every word you were about to unleash, but people like that are parasites. They feed on your reactions and then others feast on their gossip."

"You know her?" Violet asked as she attempted to pull herself together.

"No," he said. "But I know her type."

Violet rubbed her hands aimlessly on her skirt. "I don't remember her being so vicious."

His expression shifted to one of concern. "I unfortunately hear a lot of talk I don't want to hear while I'm making coffees." His next words were more delicate. "There is a story circulating about her husband and a woman with your last name—"

"My mom," she said, her words defeated. "Great."

"Her anger needs to be directed at her husband, not you. You have nothing to do with it."

Her laugh was dry. "My mother has always managed to have both nothing and everything to do with my life."

She said the words without thinking, and then saw something in Andy's gaze she didn't like. Like he felt sorry for her.

Suddenly the last few minutes settled differently in her gut. A moment ago, this tall, dark strangers' intervention had felt timely. He'd prevented an outburst she would definitely have regretted, an outburst that would've added fuel to whatever dumb gossip already circulated around Falcon about the truth of her retreat from New York.

But now... she didn't like that she'd needed his help. Over these past few months she'd dug herself a hole so deep she had no idea how she'd ever get out. But *she* needed to get out of that hole. No one had helped her back in New York. Her years of exemplary service to her employer hadn't mattered. Her two-year relationship evaporated in the blink of an eye. Her actions had caused that, and only her action could ever get her back on track again.

She didn't need a tall, dark, stranger helping her.

She didn't need anyone helping her.

"Thank you," she said, her voice now stiff. "For before. I get that you were trying to be helpful, but I want to be clear, especially as we're going to be working together – that I don't need anyone to fight my battles. I would've handled it." She shrugged. "Sure, if I'd given her that piece of my mind it would've been all over the town within an hour... but I would've handled that too."

His gaze was clear and sure. "I have no doubt."

"How? You don't know me."

His gaze flicked over her. "An educated guess."

Her lips formed into a straight line, even as she understood that her frustration was likely misdirected. "I don't need you to be my knight in shining armor," she said.

"Okay," he said, agreeably. He was back with that affable smile, a smile that didn't reach his eyes.

"I don't need saving."

"You've been very clear on that point," he said. "I made an error of judgment, and I apologize."

Now this felt all wrong, too. "You're former military, too, right?" she rushed to say. "That's your job, to protect people? You were just being nice, I get it. No need to apologize."

He leaned closer, and his smile fell away. "I own my mistakes, Violet Chapman," he said in a low voice. "Always."

For a moment she was lost in the intensity of his gaze. "Uh—"

Then he straightened, and that blinding grin was back. "So, coffee?"

THREE

He got her frustration, really.

Andy made Violet a soy milk latte – she'd asked for almond milk but they didn't have any.

She stood outside the van's window as the coffee machine whirred and the dark coffee flowed into her takeaway cup.

He didn't like people messing in his life. Particularly people who didn't know him at all – like everyone who lived in Falcon, for example. He'd lived in Philadelphia before he'd moved to Colorado, so it'd been quite the culture shock when total strangers had known his name at the grocery store, and worse – had quickly attempted to find out all his business. He hadn't provided any of it, yet much of it had been discovered. Or assumed.

He'd been cast as the former soldier with a broken heart, and to be fair he'd taken advantage of that to a point. He'd played up the supposed damage to his heart to deflect any interest from women, or more commonly –

the interest of the middle-aged matriarchs of Falcon who sniffed out eligible single men with a fervor more suited to Regency England.

He'd come to Falcon for a reason, and that was the Shadow Team. Two years ago he and the other five men he'd met that awful morning at the *Fox & Laughton* had received the same mysterious message inviting them to join something new, something that'd turned out to be a covert outside-of-the-law team of former special forces soldiers. Sometimes the team worked for hire – for governments and the world's richest organizations. And other times they worked for free for those that most needed them: the vulnerable and the desperate.

For the first year he'd worked for the Shadow Team from Philly as he'd attempted to move on from the disaster that was the end of his engagement to Natalie, and the discovery he wasn't even close to the man he'd once been. When he and Sam had worked together on an assignment, Sam had suggested a move to Falcon. Andy had agreed because, well, it was pretty damn hard living a life you could tell nobody about. Still, Falcon was never intended to be a permanent move, and he'd had no intention of becoming part of the town's community.

But Falcon didn't really give you a choice in that, as he had no doubt Violet already knew. Falcon was one giant knot of complicated entanglements, exactly what he wanted to avoid.

Yet he'd involved himself in Violet's complication. Before he'd even introduced himself, before they'd had a conversation. He watched as the soy milk frothed, his hand at the metal jug's base as he tested its temperature.

All he knew was that when the older woman had so snidely questioned Violet, his urge to help had overwhelmed him. Violet had been correct – as a Delta Force operator he absolutely was accustomed to protecting the innocent. But this was not a war zone or a Shadow Team assignment. It hadn't been life or death – it'd been a few nasty words in front of a coffee van.

He should've stayed the hell out of it, Violet was absolutely right.

It was none of his business.

He finished making her coffee and handed it out the window. Her smile was friendly as she thanked him, but she didn't meet his gaze.

She was even more beautiful up close, with the pretty freckles he'd known she'd have and the most remarkable green eyes he'd ever seen.

It seemed they were both particularly careful their fingers didn't brush.

Good.

VIOLET STARTED THE NEXT DAY. She'd toned down her work attire and simply wore jeans and a sweater as she tidied up her office. She missed her beautiful New York clothing, but had to admit wearing sneakers was a heck of a lot more comfortable. All the Cars & Coffee guys were in some mechanic's meeting in the garage, so she'd been left to her own devices. She was on her hands and knees picking up a pile of papers she'd accidentally knocked over when the office door opened. She was behind the desk, and in the few seconds it took to climb to her feet, the door clicked shut again. On a filing cabinet near the door now sat a coffee cup.

Grateful, she abandoned her tidying momentarily to collect her coffee. With one delicious sip she recognized what it was – an almond milk latte. She smiled.

Andy had remembered.

She didn't have any particular reason for drinking almond milk – no allergy, and she wasn't vegan. She just liked the taste.

She took another sip and acknowledged the sudden warmth to her cheeks had nothing to do with her hot beverage... but rather Cars & Coffee's hot barista.

She walked back to the desk, put her latte down, and took a step back. As if the latte was somehow to blame for the way Andy had affected her yesterday. She laughed as she realized what she'd done. The coffee was harmless.

Andy Torres, however... he was definitely dangerous.

If waking up naked on your company's boardroom floor – with the *married* head of IT support beside her – had taught Violet anything, it was not to mix sex with her job. Or mix a new prescription with copious alcohol. She still didn't remember much of the night that'd ruined her career – or understand how she could possibly have done something so utterly out of character - but she did know that no matter how hot Andy may be, nothing was *ever* going to happen between them.

She picked up her coffee again.

In the spirit of nothing-ever-happening-between-them – she was going to thank her new colleague for his thoughtfulness.

Outside the sun was shining, and 1980s Bon Jovi blasted from the garage as Sam and the other two mechanics worked. Cars & Coffee was only a short walk from main street, set back from a row of trees and flanked by a furniture restorer on one side and a flooring shop on the other. She'd pulled up the blind in her office to keep an eye on the comings and goings at the coffee van, and hadn't been at all surprised by Cars & Coffee's popularity. It had to be said, Falcon had been crying out for decent coffee for decades. The first thing she'd done when she'd returned home was order a serving of pancakes from Mary Lou's diner. While the pancakes had been just as wonderful as she remembered, the bitter drip coffee had near made her gag.

There was no queue at the van as she approached.

Andy saw her and rested his elbows on the counter as he smiled that easy grin that was rapidly becoming familiar.

"'Morning," he said.

She smiled back. Today his smile was genuine, while the sparkle in his hazel gaze would've taken her breath – if she'd allowed it.

"Thank you for the almond milk," she said. Rather briskly, maybe.

"Don't thank me," he said with a laconic shrug. "I'm not sure who put it in my fridge."

"But who else knows I like almond milk?"

Another shrug. "Must have been one of the guys."

Confused, she headed for the garage. She bumped into Caleb first, but he didn't know what she was talking about.

Dev rolled out from under the car he was working on when she asked him, remaining on his back on the low padded cart on wheels as he looked up at her with an irritated expression. "Do I look like I know anything about almond milk?"

"Clearly not," she said. "My apologies."

He rolled his eyes and slid back under the vehicle.

Sam walked out of the long narrow room that edged the far wall of the garage. Sam had given her a tour yesterday, so she knew that inside was a break and locker room, with a few couches, a microwave, fridge and a bathroom with a shower.

He raised his eyebrows as she approached. "Did you buy me almond milk?" she asked.

"Was that a condition of your employment?" he replied, but unlike Dev he was smiling.

"No," she said, now confused and feeling foolish. "But I appear to have a mysterious almond milk benefactor."

Sam's gaze flicked to the coffee van and then back to her. "How strange."

"Yes," she agreed, as an idea formed. "Thanks anyway."

She strode back to the van where Andy still leaned against the counter, watching her.

She narrowed her gaze. "It wasn't one of the guys."

"My mistake," he said calmly. "Terrible memory. It was me."

She huffed out a frustrated breath. "Why on Earth did you do that? All I did was waste five minutes of my time and annoy Dev."

"Nah," he said, "Two minutes that took, max. And Dev is always annoyed, you didn't make any difference."

"But *why*?" she said, exasperated. "Are you a child?"

He straightened to his full height, and her gaze was again drawn to the way the fabric of his T-shirt clung to the hardness of his shoulders. "Nope," he said easily.

"That was stupid."

"Yes," he agreed.

She gritted her teeth. "Are you always this irritating?"

Again with that affable grin.

She realized she'd stomped her foot when his gaze dropped and he raised an eyebrow.

"This is the first day of my new job," she said, "why on earth would you waste my time?"

"It's your first day of your new job," he said, "and I bought you almond milk, and I'll make sure to keep it in stock."

She blinked, as she'd temporarily forgotten his original kindness.

"That *was* nice of you," she began. "Thank you—"

"No big deal," he interrupted. "Everyone who works at Cars & Coffee gets their preferred hot beverage each day."

"Of course," she said, thrown once again by his

matter-of-factness. "I still don't get the wild goose chase thing."

He leaned over the counter so they were closer to eye level. "All the guys do harmless, stupid shit like that to each other. Once Sam hid my truck for no fucking reason. And there was the time Caleb mucked around with Dev's predictive text on his phone, so normal words like *and* and *yes* autocorrected to *snuffleupagus*. Dev's not all that tech-savvy, so that took him ages to fix."

Despite herself, she giggled imagining grumpy Dev desperately trying to fix his cell.

"See?" he said. "You're part of the team now. Stupid shit will happen occasionally."

She held his gaze, suddenly understanding the subtext. "You'll treat me just like Sam, Dev or Caleb."

He nodded. For a moment they both seemed to acknowledge the tension between them. The tension that'd been there right from the beginning, regardless of old English teachers or almond milk. And the tension that clearly neither of them were going to explore. "Exactly," he said.

For a moment her stomach dropped as she wondered at his reasons for establishing this boundary, and as she acknowledged her unwanted disappointment.

"Good," she said firmly.

It's good, she reminded herself as she walked across the lot to the office, her almond milk latte still warm against her palm.

Good.

. . .

A WEEK LATER, Andy arrived at Cars & Coffee – first in, as always – to the interior of the coffee van wallpapered in hundreds of photocopies of the same circa 1990s image of Nicholas Cage.

He burst into laughter. Violet had surprised him.

"Why Nick Cage?" he asked Violet when she walked over with her new travel cup for her morning almond latte an hour later. She'd stuck to casual clothing ever since her interview. Today she wore faded skinny jeans and a UChicago sweater, and her hair was in a high ponytail that swung when she walked. She looked hot, but then – she always did. She'd been wearing this exact pair of ass-hugging skinny jeans when he'd impulsively pranked her about her almond milk. With her ass looking that good, categorizing her as *just one of the boys* with his dumb joke had been a wise – he'd thought - reminder to himself.

"It's called 'Caging'," she said with a grin, looking extremely pleased with herself. "I liked the randomness of it. Google has been super helpful, I've got dozens of ideas now."

Over the next few weeks they went back and forth with dumb shit.

Andy taped a small picture of himself to the sensor of her computer mouse so when she eventually turned it over in frustration after attempting to connect and reconnect the useless device, he got the satisfaction of her exasperated shriek – heard right across the parking lot.

One morning during the largest coffee crowd of school moms and retirees, Violet appeared with a tray of beautifully iced cupcakes, and soon had the whole crowd singing him *Happy Birthday*. She'd stood beside him, singing enthusiastically out of tune as he'd glowered in silence.

It had not been his birthday.

A couple of months after Violet started, she stepped outside her Nanna's house to her Prius entirely covered in post-it notes. He'd had to man both the office phone and the van for an hour that morning, but it was totally worth it for her thunderous expression when she finally arrived at work.

"What a waste of perfectly good post-its," she'd said. She loved the things.

That'd been a Friday, and that night at The Roost, Falcon's only bar, Sam looked at him with some speculation. "Things okay with Vi?" he asked.

The bar was buzzing around them. Friday night at The Roost was a Falcon institution, and while initially they'd all been dragged along by Sam's force-of-nature sister Casey, to be honest they now all enjoyed the chance to unwind each week. If you weren't on a Shadow Team job, you were at The Roost on a Friday, no excuses.

Dev was on assignment in Texas, retrieving vital evidence for a particularly nasty stalking situation, so it was just Sam, Andy and Caleb tonight. Violet and Casey sat on the far side of the bar deep in conversation. Andy didn't even think Violet had noticed him arrive.

"Why wouldn't they be?" Andy replied.

"That gossip from New York is doing the rounds again."

Andy nodded. He'd heard it too – and had swiftly shut down any talk about Violet's supposedly scandalous night in her employer's boardroom whenever he overheard it near the coffee van. He thought back to the day they'd met and that vicious ex-teacher, or even the way she went toe to toe with him with their pranks. Or how she lifted her chin and ignored any gossip about her mom, which unfortunately wasn't all that uncommon at The Roost. "She's cool, I'm sure she's got it handled."

"Cool, hey?" Caleb rolled his eyes. "You can just ask her out, you know. No more of this flirtation via practical joke."

"Since when did I want your opinion on my personal life, Grey?"

Sam frowned. "It's already a risk having Violet working for us. If you get too close, she might start asking questions."

Caleb snorted. "Ha! *Get too close* is a weird way of describing what Violet and Torres want to do to each other."

"Watch it, Grey," Andy warned.

Caleb rolled his eyes again.

Andy drained the rest of his beer and relaxed against the bar. "There's nothing going on between Violet and I." When he heard Violet's familiar laugh somewhere amongst the hub-bub of the bar it took more effort than he'd like to keep his attention focused on the two men beside him.

"I don't care about your personal life, Torres," Sam said. "You do you, I give zero fucks. But – I do care about

Cars & Coffee." *And the Shadow Team.* That bit didn't need to be said. "Be careful, and maybe lay off all the pranks? One or two is one thing, but this is getting juvenile. You're in your thirties, man."

Conversation moved on quickly. The Shadow Team wasn't really about having serious conversations. Andy believed Sam when he said he didn't care about his personal life, and he knew Sam wouldn't care if he asked Violet out – as long as he didn't do anything stupid and reveal what Cars & Coffee really was. Or do anything stupid and hurt Violet – Cars & Coffee would be a mess if they lost her. She ran the place as well-oiled as the engines they fixed, leaving them free to focus on the Shadow Team.

But the pranks comment?

Andy was the first of the Shadow Team to leave The Roost that night, and he headed straight to Trader Joe's. When Sam left an hour or so later, it was to find his truck almost entirely wrapped in clingfilm.

Juvenile yes. Funny – also yes.

Violet had noticed Andy arrive.

One moment she'd been focused on Casey's animated re-telling of how she'd stumbled across a tryst behind the Social Sciences shelves at the Falcon County library where she volunteered – and the next there'd been Andy.

Tall, with his mussed hair, grey denim jeans and a black sweater that managed to not be tight while also clinging to his muscular chest *just right.* He wasn't looking at her. He was laughing at something Caleb was saying as they walked into the bar, absolutely oblivious to where she and Casey perched on their bar stools.

"And to be fair," Casey continued, "I say *well done them*, because honestly – when I'm in my sixties I absolutely aspire to being felt up while reading a comparative politics textbook." She paused and swiveled on her bar stool to look over her shoulder. "Who are *you* practically drooling at?" she asked.

Violet's gaze snapped down to her drink. She glared at the slice of orange in her cocktail as she shook her head. "Oh, no one," she said. She'd aimed for breezy, but instead sounded defensive. *Damnit.*

Casey cleared her throat. "Be careful," she said. "Andy Torres has quite the reputation."

Violet looked up. "I didn't say it was Andy."

Casey rolled her eyes. The woman's wavy bob swished against her jaw as she wiggled on her seat. Violet had noticed Casey was rarely perfectly still. "It was Andy. He's the only Cars & Coffee employee you've been engaging in prank foreplay with."

Violet gasped. "It is *not* prank..." she whispered the last bit, "...*foreplay.*" She swallowed and straightened her shoulders. "I just shared a couple of amusing...anecdotes with you. I could easily have told you about silly stuff that...*Dev* did, or something."

Casey raised an eyebrow. Dev was possibly a poor choice of example. She didn't think she'd ever seen the guy smile.

"I - I just didn't let him get away with pranking me. We only do it because we're treating each other like *one of the guys*. Andy even said it like that."

Casey's snort was loud enough to draw attention. "Vi, I'm only just starting to get to know you, but my bullshit-o-meter is never wrong."

Violet tipped the rest of her cocktail down her throat, then plonked her drink on the bar's oak countertop. "It's not—" she began, then sighed as she ran a hand through her hair. She wore it out tonight, carefully curled in soft dark-red waves. She'd even worn her fancy glasses, the ones with rose-gold arms and a hint of a cats-eye tilt. Her silky cream shirt had a deep vee, and she'd worn pink velvet pumps with her pale blue jeans. As she'd gotten ready, she'd told herself it was because it was her first night at *The Roost*, an institution she'd avoided since her return – but after her third invitation from Casey she'd run out of excuses. Especially given Casey's reasoning:

Friday's my mom hosts games-a-palooza at the ranch. Please save me from a choice between playing banana-grams and hanging out with my brother on my one kid-free night of the week.

So, all this effort was because she wanted to put her best pink-velvet-pump clad foot forward to the people of Falcon, and for Casey, too. Casey Taberner had been effortlessly popular in high school, and even all these years later Violet had to admit she found her a little intimidating. Casey was all the things Violet hadn't been at school: smart, wealthy and respected.

Violet still didn't know why Casey was being so nice

to her. One short conversation in front of the freezer cases at Trader Joes and she had a job with Casey's brother, they'd had a coffee catchup at Mary Lou's, and then three subsequent invitations to hang out at The Roost before she'd finally agreed tonight.

Casey had gone above and beyond any standard for small-town welcome, and while Violet still felt a little uncomfortable in the face of Casey's determined kindness, it did feel real.

For that reason, and because she'd decided to stop lying to herself about why she'd dressed so carefully tonight, she changed direction. "Whether or not it's foreplay – which it *isn't* - is a moot point. Yes, I've noticed Andy Torres is... *attractive.* But I'm not interested in dating him for many reasons." On the far side of the U-shaped bar, Andy and the other men were ordering drinks. But Violet made sure to pay no attention as she focused on Casey. "Having said that, I'm keen to know of any *other* reasons why I shouldn't date him. Like this reputation you mentioned."

Violet knew her interest in this information was utterly transparent. *Whatever*. She *was* interested.

Casey frowned at her over the rim of her beer glass. "Hmmm," she said. "Well, I guess that's good news. I mean, he's a good guy, I think, fundamentally. From what Sam has said, and just from hanging out a bit at the garage with my girls. He's really nice to my daughters and that's always a good sign." She took a sip of her beer. "But, a friend of Amanda Travelli's cousin in Denver – do you remember Mandy from Falcon High? She's doing so well with her lawncare business." She didn't wait for Violet to respond. "Anyway. Mandy's cousin's friend hooked up with Andy after she watched him *fight* in Boulder."

"Fight?" Violet raised a surprised, worried hand to her mouth.

"Yeah, boxing. Amateur fights, but he's pretty good by all accounts. Seems to win a lot. But win or lose, he's on the hunt after a fight. Now the women aren't complaining, but he's become so notorious it's become a thing."

"A thing?"

"Yeah. They say he um... fights, fucks and flees. That's his thing."

"Oh," Violet said.

"Yeah. Oh."

Violet's hand fell from her mouth as she brushed non-existent fluff from her jeans nonchalantly. "There's nothing *wrong* with that if he's honest and...safe, I guess."

She didn't like the curl of heavy jealousy in her gut.

"Of course," Casey said briskly. "No slut shaming here."

"No," Violet agreed. "He can fight, fuck and flee to his heart's content. I don't care."

Her new friend looked skeptical, but still nodded. "Good." Then she added, "the rumor is Andy's like that because of a bad breakup. He was engaged, and from the little Sam says I think it was pretty messy."

"Okay," Violet said. She lay her palms flat on her thighs as she took a breath. "So, you're saying should I be in need of a hook up – which to be clear, I'm not looking for just yet – I just need to head for wherever The Communist Manifesto is shelved?"

"Absolutely," Casey agreed. "Just make sure I'm not working, first."

They both laughed.

Then Casey leaned forward. "Hey, if you ever want to talk about whatever went down in New York, about what brought you back to Falcon – I'm here, okay?"

Violet chewed her bottom lip. Those same words from almost anyone else here in Falcon would've been nothing more than a shameless effort to mine for gossip. But Violet believed that Casey was genuine. Why wouldn't she be? The single mom was genuine in literally everything else she did, living her life with no filter. Still, Violet hesitated.

"Thanks," she said. "But I'm fine." A brief pause. "Another drink?"

FOUR

Andy hadn't been at work for three days, and Violet didn't like that she'd been counting.

Caleb and Sam had taken turns in the coffee van, and she'd helped out with orders on a busier day, so everything continued to run smoothly without him. In her almost three months at Cars & Coffee she'd become used to the unusual rostering schedule, and clearly Dev, Caleb and Sam took it all in stride. In fact, it was rare all four men were ever working together on the same day. She knew Caleb had regular study days for the college degree he was doing online, but she wasn't game to ask standoffish Dev what he did on his days off. She and Andy rarely spoke when they weren't doing their silly pranks, but now she assumed he was off fighting... and probably the fucking and fleeing bit too. She wished she hadn't known. Concern, she'd decided, was a normal emotion to have towards a colleague potentially having his nose broken or worse. Any hint of jealousy, however, she instantly shoved aside.

She thought it was cool what Sam was doing in creating such a flexible workplace for himself and his friends. Through Casey, she knew the men had a shared trauma from their special forces career: a siege at a hotel she remembered being in the news three or four years ago. She knew no more detail than that, but it was enough for her not to press Sam with her ideas for an online rostering system, or a way she could better juggle bookings and the men's haphazard schedule. The fact was it wasn't taking her long to streamline the business-side of Cars & Coffee, so she *did* have time to reorganize whatever needed reorganizing whenever Dev, Sam, Caleb or Andy were suddenly unavailable.

But this was the longest Andy had been absent, and she itched to ask after him. But that was the other unusual thing about Cars & Coffee – no-one talked about their lives outside of work. Usually that suited her just fine, as she had no interest in talking about New York. But today, well, it was annoying.

As a distraction she lost herself in one of her favorite things – spreadsheets. She loved playing with data, and entirely lost track of time when she was absorbed in this type of work. Today she was calculating new profit margins if they switched suppliers on several of their stock parts – things like spark plugs. Before she'd arrived all of this had been managed in a series of notebooks, the same way Sam's father had once done it. But that method meant no one really had any clue about Cars & Coffee's inventory or stock levels at any point in time – but now Violet did. She had it down to every last oil filter or head-lamp bulb.

She emerged from her office a couple of hours later to locate Sam, a print out of her latest numbers in her hand. It was late afternoon, and the coffee van was closed up for the day. Today it was 90s R&B pumping through the garage, although only one car was up on a lift at the moment. Outside Dev was talking to a customer beside an SUV, and Violet paused as she realized Andy's truck was parked alongside her Prius on the far side of the lot. Her tummy lightened knowing he was nearby, and now *that* annoyed her. She didn't want to react like this to a man she worked with.

She straightened her shoulders. She was out here to find Sam, not Andy.

With Dev clearly busy, she headed into the garage. No one was there, so she walked to the breakout room. The door was open, as usual, and she stepped inside.

"Sam?"

The space was empty. There was a row of hooks along one wall where the guys hung their jackets or back-packs or whatever. Sam's bag wasn't there – it was an ancient high school gym bag with the Falcon High Mascot – a hornet – printed on the side, so it was instantly recognizable. Instead only a folded navy-blue towel and a duffle bag sat on the bench below. She went to leave when she realized she could hear the shower running.

A moment later it stopped.

Her gaze flicked from the towel, to the door of the small bathroom and back – and before she could compute that the shower-er had clearly forgotten their towel, the bathroom door opened.

And Andy Torres walked out. Completely naked.

She gasped in horror.

Well, to be fair – horror wasn't all that accurate. Shocked, yes – but in the split second her gaze had taken in the sight of Andy and his golden, glorious, muscular self before she slapped her hand over her eyes – the view had been far from horrible.

"Sorry!" she squeaked. "I was just looking for Sam."

"Well, he wasn't in the shower with me," Andy said dryly.

Violet laughed despite herself.

"Now that isn't all that flattering," he continued. There was a rustle of movement. "I'm decent now."

She dropped her hand, feeling foolish. Why hadn't she just walked out of the room?

As she looked at Andy wearing a towel low on his hips, she had her answer. She hadn't wanted to.

He was looking at her. Properly, like he had that first morning outside the van, and not at all like the last few months, where they'd communicated with silly pranks and the shortest of conversations. Barely – she realized now – even glancing at each other.

So now, with the full force of Andy Torres' attention on her, it was... all consuming.

She'd pretended the delicious tension from the first 24 hours they'd known each other had dissipated, but that was clearly nothing more than denial. Now, her skin was hot, and her belly was liquid. He was utterly, utterly gorgeous, from his shaggy dark hair, to his powerful body, to his many, many tattoos. He even had a few wrapped around one thigh, she now knew.

How could she ever work with him again without thinking of that? Thinking of the art that hugged his body, thinking of how she now knew he had only a smattering of hair on his chest, thinking that she now knew what was between his thighs.

He was studying her, too. It was summer, so she wore denim shorts, an untucked white shirt, and pink converse sneakers that matched her glasses. She was decidedly *not* naked, yet the intensity of his gaze stripped her bare.

He looked his fill as he travelled from her lips, to her breasts, her hips, and her legs.

Her skin grew warmer, hotter, with every moment that passed.

Slowly, his attention wandered back up, and by the time their gazes locked again, she couldn't begin to remember why she'd decided nothing could ever happen with this man. Was she insane? Why had she kept her distance? She'd never felt like this before. She'd never felt this primal need to touch a man. Or this desperate need for that man to touch her.

She took a step towards him before she realized what she was doing. The next two steps were deliberate.

"Andy—" she said, her voice low and breathy.

But he didn't move.

"Stop," he said firmly. Clearly. "I'm not interested."

His clipped words were like a bucket of iced water tipped over her.

"Pardon me?"

She had *not* imagined the way he'd been looking at her. She had not imagined the instant and now months-long spark between them.

"You heard what I said," he said. Then he added more gently. "Sorry."

"*Sorry?*"

She shook her head, completely disoriented. "What are you going on about, Andy?"

She hurriedly took three steps back and hugged herself. He didn't reply, he just looked at her.

But he was looking at her with that impenetrable gaze he wore whenever his smile didn't reach his eyes. He was giving her nothing.

She opened her mouth, then snapped it shut. What was she going to do? Argue?

He'd been brutally clear.

Now it was humiliation that pinkened her cheeks and made her all hot and bothered. *Had* she imagined it? With every passing second doubt began to cloud her previous certainty. After all, this wouldn't be the first time in recent history where something she'd been *sure* about – something she would've staked her life on – had been wrong.

"I didn't come in here on purpose," she said, her rushed apologetic tone reminding her of the panic she'd felt in New York when she'd realized how wrong she'd been. "I'm not some pervert."

"I know that," he said. *Kindly*. He said it kindly.

Tears prickled. And they weren't about Andy, not at all. They were about what had happened in New York, where her gut had been wrong and her life had collapsed on top of her. This wasn't a disaster. Andy Torres saying no to her wasn't a disaster.

Five minutes ago, she hadn't even *wanted* anything with him.

God, she was way too good at lying to herself.

Pride straightened her shoulders and halted those unwelcome tears.

"I'll leave you to it," she said.

She walked stiffly back to the office. Ironically Sam was in there, looking for her.

Somehow she was able to walk him through her figures, and then he was gone.

She sat at her desk and dropped her forehead to the wooden surface.

She gave herself a minute to let Andy's rejection wash over her in a wave of embarrassment.

Then she sat up and made a decision.

No more flirtation disguised as pranks, no more worrying about Andy when he wasn't here. No more treating Andy any differently to Sam, Dev or Caleb.

Torres.

That's what the other men called him. Sam was Tabs, Dev was Dev, and Caleb was Grey.

Torres.

She'd use that from now on, so when she said his

name she wasn't reminded of her breathy little plea in the break room.

There was a knock on her open office door. It was Andy, now fully dressed. She didn't allow herself to work out what his expression meant. It definitely wasn't *nothing* anymore.

"Torres," she said firmly, her attention on her computer screen. "Can it wait? I've got a few orders to get sorted before close of business."

"Torres," he repeated to himself, nodding as he looked out the window to the coffee van. His gaze swung back to her. "It's nothing," he said. "It's not important."

She let out a breath as he walked away.

But when she looked down at all the data she'd shown Sam, the numbers remained blurry until she'd blinked away her unshed tears.

FIVE

Andy's assignment had been in Europe, a relatively straightforward job to transport highly sensitive design documents from Paris to Berlin for a billionaire entrepreneur. The de-brief had been equally straightforward as the job had been utterly uneventful. He'd left the secure teleconference with Shadow Operations slightly early, leaving Tabs and Grey to discuss their upcoming assignments. As he always did, he carefully checked the camera-feed to ensure Violet – or anyone else – didn't witness his exit from the hidden armory and communications center hidden behind the Cars & Coffee break room. But the screens revealed Violet's Prius was no longer in the lot. She'd finished for the day.

He felt a twinge of... something that she wasn't there. Had he hoped she still would be? But why? Half an hour ago she'd called him *Torres* for the first time. Ten minutes before that he'd forced himself to say: *I'm not interested.*

Both were a good thing. He'd made their situation

clear, and she'd subsequently put even further distance between them by using the name the Shadow Team called him. She'd understood, she'd made that clear.

He walked towards his truck.

He'd hurt Violet.

That bit he hadn't intended. In fact, none of it he'd intended. How could he have planned her walking in on him butt-naked? But when she had, and when he'd reacted to her the way he had... he'd had to end it. That pull between them as he'd worn a towel and she'd stood there in her cute-as-fuck pink sneakers with her hot-as-fuck long legs... it'd been so damn intense it had taken literally all he had to not yank her into his arms and shove her up against the wall.

He gripped his truck's door handle for a long moment as need washed over him once again. How did Violet do that to him? She wasn't even here and he was getting a semi. Fuck's sake.

He got into his truck and drove home.

He was renting a small townhouse a short drive from Cars & Coffee. It was a completely generic building, but the street was nice enough, with lots of trees and of course the Rocky Mountains as a backdrop. More importantly it had a double garage. He parked his truck on one side, leaving the other for his boxing bag and speed ball. Today, as soon as the garage door slid shut he was out of his car and tugging on his boxing gloves. Moments later he was redirecting his unwanted sexual urges into what he was good at: violence. He pummeled that boxing bag until he was soaked with sweat. Punch after punch after punch.

But tonight, this urge to hit *something* did not result in its usual outcome. It didn't result in that perfect laser focus, where his concentration narrowed down to how he could direct his body in the most effective, powerful way. When he had an opponent, his focus was on identifying the target for his next blow. On identifying another man's weaknesses.

When it was just him and this bag, it was about losing himself in the movement of his own bone and muscle. Losing himself in the harshness of his breathing and in the pounding of his heart until his mind was blank with the delicious ache of pushing himself to his physical limit.

But with every swing of his fists, his brain remained perfectly clear and focused on one thing: *Violet.*

For the first time since he'd walked in on Natalie with another man, with-

He stepped back from the bag, gasping for breath.

For the first time since he'd learned to direct his violence at a punching bag or a willing opponent, the rhythm of boxing did not help.

He ripped off his gloves and headed upstairs for a shower.

As the ice-cold water collided with muscles still hot and screaming from his exertions, he leaned his forearm, and then his forehead, against the cool tiles.

What the actual fuck was wrong with him?

For months now he'd been content in his situation with Violet: that there was no situation. They were colleagues who occasionally pranked each other, nothing more.

Liar. Had he ever painstakingly planned a prank on Sam, or Dev or Grey with a buzz of anticipation low in his gut? Absolutely not. He'd already fucking bought hundreds of balloons and a helium pump in preparation for filling her office to the roof with balloons for her birthday, which was still another month away. He'd even picked the balloon colors based on the glasses she wore in rotation.

He gritted his teeth as his body cooled and the icy beat of the shower became increasingly uncomfortable.

It physically hurt him that he'd hurt her.

It twisted his gut. If Falcon had its own boxing gym where he could put himself in the ring to have the shit beat out of him, he would've done it. He deserved that for the shocked humiliation he'd caused Violet. She'd been embarrassed, yet she had no reason to be. He did want her. He was interested.

But he couldn't have her.

He pushed away from the wall and twisted the faucets off before roughly grabbing a towel to dry himself. Then he quickly dressed and went back to his car.

He knew what the gossips of Falcon said he did: Fight, Fuck and Flee.

Well, he might not be able to fight tonight, but surely a fuck would get Violet out of his brain? A fuck just like he liked it, and just like he had no doubt would horrify Violet Chapman: raw, and rough and with zero emotion involved. Just pleasure. Pure, mind-numbing pleasure.

He drove the two hours to Denver to find it.

CASEY INVITED Violet and her grandmother to the Taberner ranch for morning tea on Sunday morning.

It was shrewd of Casey, Violet had to admit. As much as Violet liked Casey, she still felt awkward around her. Violet's persona in New York, or even in Chicago, had been confident and accomplished. She'd never been one to have dozens of friends, but she *had* had a small friendship circle. Here in Falcon, she'd never had that. She'd been a Chapman first, and Violet second. At high school a mix of her family heritage – and her obnoxious behavior to live up to that heritage – meant she'd had no close friends growing up. Even now, a handful of months into living in her home town she felt like a fish out of water.

"Honestly Violet, if you can think of a good reason why you would deny your sweet nanna a slice of my mom's famous apple pie, I'll just about give up on you," Casey had said.

This had been on Friday night, two days after Andy's humiliating rejection. She hadn't mentioned it to Casey, but she had drunk more than usual. Maybe that was why she'd accepted the invitation? Or maybe the buzz of alcohol had allowed her past her own bullshit?

After all, why was she resisting Casey's friendship? Why was she being weird?

Despite all that, she still felt out of place on Sunday morning as she sat in the spacious dining room of the

Taberner ranch. It wasn't a working ranch, with the only livestock a furry pony belonging to Casey's daughters. But the house was grand and lovely, with high ceilings and sweeping views of rolling fields edged with white fence. Her nanna was having a great time, charming Casey's mom Roberta with childhood memories of Roberta's late mother. Rose Chapman may be in her 80s, but she was as sharp as a tack. At one end of the long table Casey's daughters Amber and Annabelle were busy with coloring books, occasionally holding up their work for praise from the adults.

"Violet," Amber said, "which is better, mine or Annabelle's?" The older of the two girls held up her own drawing before snatching up her sisters.

"Hey!" Annabelle yelled. "I'm not finished!"

"Doesn't matter," Amber said seriously. "My superior talent should already be obvious." She met Violet's gaze. "Right, Violet?"

"Uh—"

"Right, Violet?" her nanna repeated.

"Pardon me?" Violet asked, feeling a little panicked as she turned to her Nanna beside her. Surely, she wasn't supposed to *actually* choose? "I'm not sure I'm a qualified judge of coloring in."

Now her nanna frowned. "Coloring in? No. I'm talking about how with you being such a wiz with numbers, you would just love to be on the Falcon County Fair & Rodeo committee."

Utterly thrown, Violet gaped at her.

Casey clapped her hands. "Yes! Great idea. And it

will be just the thing to make Violet feel like part of the Falcon community again."

Again? That would imply she once had been.

"I'm not sure I have the time to give the Rodeo the amount of attention it deserves," she said carefully. "I'm very busy in my role at the garage—"

"Pfft!" Rose said. "I have no doubt you work *extremely* hard at Cars & Coffee." The older woman looked first at Roberta, then Casey – as if both would report back to Sam on her dedication to her employer – then more firmly back at Violet. "But that's all you do, sweetie. You have acres of spare time now you've finished re-organizing my house." Her grandmother clasped her hands to her heart. "Honestly, Roberta, you should see what she's done to my spice drawer. And my pantry!"

Violet felt her cheeks grow hot.

Her nanna's expression was sharp, but also full of concern. What she'd told Rose about New York had been light on detail, but her grandmother knew enough to know how devastated Violet was by the damage to her career. And also, by the damage to her confidence.

Back home in Falcon she supposed she'd become somewhat of an automaton – heading to work and back, resisting almost all Casey's efforts to socialize, and otherwise rarely leaving the house. Her silly prank-communication with Andy – which she now knew, absolutely, was *not* foreplay, had been the one spark of interest in her life.

His rejection still felt raw, and now even more pathetic.

"I'll think about it," Violet conceded. Then she

thought back to her old English teacher from her first day at Cars & Coffee. No one else had been so bold, but her MBA and her New York heels didn't stop her being Iris Chapman's daughter, and she'd felt the interested stares, and heard the murmured whispers at Trader Joes, or simply walking down main street.

Later Rose and Roberta headed outside to watch the girls play beneath the shade of an oak tree. Violet carried a small pile of plates to the sink while Casey squirted dishwashing liquid into it.

"Why did you invite me over today?" Violet asked abruptly. "And out for coffee last week? And The Roost on Fridays?"

Casey picked up a dirty saucer and scrubbed at it with a sponge before glancing up. "Because we're friends?"

"But why?" Violet pushed. She picked up a dishcloth.

Casey took a step back from the sink and looked at Violet. "Why not? You've just moved back to Falcon." She shrugged. "I moved back to Falcon only recently too, after my divorce. It was harder than I thought settling back in."

Violet nodded. Casey hadn't shared much about her ex-husband, other than to refer to him as "the asshole".

"You're being nice," Violet said. She shook her head. "Of course you're being nice. *You're* nice. Ignore me and my weird questions."

Casey gave a burst of laughter. "I'm only being nice because I like you, Vi. I'm not the self-appointed Falcon welcoming committee." She grinned. "I always thought you were a cool kid. I'm glad for you that you went to college and had your high-flying career, but I always admired the way you kinda burned everything down at high school. Because I babysat you in middle school I knew how smart you were, and I never believed you were going to turn out like your mom. I was pretty sure it was all an act, but you were goddamn convincing." She paused. "I thought you were so brave."

"Brave?" Violet gave a laugh of surprise. "For petty theft and half-assing school?"

"For giving the town the finger for judging you."

Violet swallowed. "Oh," she said.

"See? Brave." Her lips quirked. "Meanwhile I was too scared to be anything but perfect."

"I thought you *were* perfect," Violet said.

This time Casey's laugh had a brittle edge. "This is feeling a little heavy for washing-up conversation." She straightened her shoulders. "But are you over your *why-are-you-being-nice-to-me* bullshit?"

Violet nodded. "Yes. From now on I'll only reject your invitations when I genuinely don't want to spend time with you."

Now Casey's laugh was sincere. "That's the spirit."

ANDY WOKE UP, alone, just before noon on Sunday.

He scrubbed at his eyes as he rolled away from the unwanted slivers of sunlight that determinedly pushed through the cracks in his closed blinds.

His head hurt from too much bourbon, but his body

ached from several satisfying rounds of sparring at a boxing gym just outside of Vail. The bourbon had been consumed at a trendy basement bar in Vail itself that leaned hard into the town's tourist-vibe. The place had been packed with tourists, even in Summer, and it *should've* been exactly what he'd needed. At first it had been – he'd arrived alone, struck up a conversation with a very attractive blonde woman, and fallen right into the rhythm he hadn't been able to find in Denver two days earlier. In Denver he hadn't even finished his drink before heading home, telling himself it was jetlag that caused his utter apathy in pursuing any of the clearly interested women in his vicinity, and not the memory of Violet's humiliation when he'd rejected her.

He hadn't had that excuse last night, but he'd failed just the same.

He and the blonde had flirted easily. He'd said the right things, and so had she. She'd invited him to leave with her, and then she'd tugged him into a shopfront alcove on the walk to her hotel.

The moment her lips touched his he knew it wasn't going to work. He'd kissed her back with some half-formed idea that he just needed to warm up, but it was all totally wrong.

Even the woman's assertiveness was wrong. *He* should be the one dragging giggling women into dark corners to make them feel fucking good. *He* should be the one in charge. That was what he'd become these last few years. Sex wasn't playful for him anymore; it was direct and straight to the point.

Not...this. This passive, uninterested dude with a dick that couldn't be any more flaccid.

He'd extracting himself from the woman's embrace, apologized and found a sports bar that kept the bourbons coming until it was clear his truck would be spending the night in Vail.

He pushed himself out of bed and headed for the shower. Surely a blast of cold water would clear his head of this bullshit.

He'd done the right thing.

Better for Violet to be hurt now than later. At least all he'd done to her was bruise her ego.

She must never learn how capable he was of inflicting pain.

SIX

The Roost

Falcon, Colorado.

Present day

Violet stood in the alley beside The Roost, her back pressed against the brick wall as she took several deep breaths.

She stared up at the sky and its pretty puffs of whispery clouds as she contemplated what a complete and utter idiot she was.

What the fuck is wrong with me?

She wasn't one to curse all that often, but this situation warranted it. Nearly a whole year she'd been back home in Falcon. A year that'd been nothing like what she'd expected.

No, that wasn't true.

Some stuff had gone exactly to script – in that her mother still only spoke to her to ask for money.

But that, she could manage.

What she hadn't expected was to....not despise living here? This place she'd been so desperate to leave, and that she'd so desperately hated. And she didn't even feel that was an exaggeration. She'd *hated* Falcon. Or more accurately – the way the place had made her feel.

Worthless.

Useless.

And if she thought to much about her mostly absent mother: *Unlovable.*

She dug her nails into her palms to distract herself from a familiar ache in her chest, then shook her head. That wasn't the point right now.

The point was she was back in Falcon and despite gossip of her New York scandal spreading through town within days of her return – causing some folks to double down on all of Violet's teenage labels – not everyone was like that. She had a handful of friends, a job she liked, and an only slightly grudging appreciation for the town community now she'd agreed to help the rodeo committee manage their finances. She'd even saved enough money to consider trying to break back into her old career in a new city, with a few job applications half-written. All great, right?

Except one thing.

Sex.

She was thirty years old and she hadn't had sex in a year. There'd been no one since Matt, her software engineer ex-boyfriend who'd instantly – and understandably – dumped her once she'd tearfully told him exactly why she'd been fired from Curtis Pharmaceuticals.

And Violet...missed it.

She missed everything about it. Even with Matt, who hadn't always been the most generous of lovers. She missed the intimacy, the kisses, and the soft laughter. She missed the sheer pleasure in being *taken.*

She bit her lip and her eyes slid closed.

For a moment she couldn't hear the muffled sounds of the bar through the wall, or the sounds of Main Street. Instead, she imagined the murmur of a man's voice in her ear, and the touch of large hands on her skin. Her belly tightened and her cheeks grew hot as she imagined hot kisses trailing down her neck, and sure, clever fingers between her legs.

Then in that little fantasy, she opened her eyes and saw the man that was making her feel so good.

Andy Torres.

Her eyes snapped open. "Fuck!"

The single word burst out in the silence of the alley, startling a matronly woman walking past on Main Street who tsked disapprovingly despite Violet's swift "Sorry!"

Adding another person to the list of people who disapproved of the Chapman women was not of Violet's concern. Her inability to think about sex without her subconscious conjuring up the most irritating, infuriating man in the world, was.

Andy was why she hadn't had sex in a year.

Violet gripped the phone in her hand tightly. Ten

minutes ago the guy she'd been dating after meeting him at the Tipsy Tree in Denver had called her. She'd seen his name pop up on her cell phone as she'd walked from her Prius to The Roost to meet Casey, and she'd been pleased. Because after two perfectly pleasant dates and a kiss that definitely had potential, she'd decided this guy was *it*. The guy she'd end this inexplicable celibacy streak with. Because he was the third very nice guy she'd dated in the past twelve months, and enough was enough. This time she was *not* going to do something super dumb like with Guy Number One – an accountant – who she'd been making out with on his overstuffed sofa only to sigh: *Andy*. That had been bad enough, but the accountant had laughed it off. When she'd done it again two minutes later, he'd suggested they put a pause on their relationship until she was able to remember the name of the guy with his hand up her shirt.

She'd dismissed that as dating too soon after the New York nightmare, and maybe a smidge too close to Andy's humiliating rejection.

The next guy she'd met three months later. He'd actually come into Cars & Coffee to pick up his mother's car, although he lived a few towns over. They went for burgers at Mary Lou's Diner one night, then seen a movie in Edwards for their second date. He seemed a decent enough guy, yet she'd declined his invitation for a third date. They just didn't click, she'd told him – and herself.

Her conversation five minutes ago with Tim from the Tipsy Tree had been along the same lines: *It was fun, but if I'm honest I'm not seeing a future together.*

Then he'd made her laugh when he'd asked: *No worries. How about just sex, then?*

Tim was a handsome guy. Tall, fit, successful. He was exactly the kind of guy she would usually go for. Yet, he did nothing for her. None of the men she'd dated had done *anything* for her. The only thing that made her skin hot and her belly liquid was when her wayward brain superimposed Andy in their place.

Andy. Fucking. Torres.

Maybe Violet cursed more often than she thought.

She pushed away from the wall and headed for The Roost's entrance. She was being ridiculous. In the nine months since Torres had walked out of that shower butt naked, her relationship with the former Delta Force operator had settled into one of barbed banter. Initially she'd tried to ignore him, but when Torres had insisted on delivering her daily latte to her office despite her efforts to avoid his coffee van, she'd decided she'd simply be polite. But he hadn't liked her succinct politeness, and had attempted to be blandly charming.

That had rubbed her the wrong way, as she'd instantly recognized the tone he used to harmlessly flirt with the school moms.

"Could you not?" she'd said sharply, looking up from her desk after she'd thanked him for her coffee and he'd started telling her some silly story about Caleb and his propensity to be late for everything.

The moment she spoke she'd wanted to snatch back the words.

He'd held up his hands in mock defense and made a

quick exit, but that was that. It started a pattern where Violet found herself irritated by everything Andy did, and somehow unable to make any effort to hide her irritation. Then one day Andy muttered something about her having a *stick up her ass* when she'd marched over to the coffee van to ask him *politely* why he hadn't been following her new stocktaking procedures... and something had shifted. The irritation became mutual. No more bland charm from Andy, no more veiled politeness from her.

From then on, every conversation prickled with antagonism.

Unless she was alone in her bedroom. *Unless* she reached for the second drawer in her nightstand.

Unless she attempted to kiss another man.

Then it was *all* Andy. It was all heat and need and vivid memories of tattoos wrapped around muscular thighs and exactly what Andy Torres had between them.

So. No sex in a year.

And it was all Andy's fault.

She walked up the steps and into the bar.

ANDY FELT DAMN GOOD.

He'd won an amateur boxing tournament today. First bout had been a unanimous points decision, then in the final the ref had stopped the contest after Andy landed so many flush punches it was clear his opponent was outclassed. His opponent had got one good left hook in though, leaving a graze along his cheekbone.

Andy had to say, one benefit of unexpected celibacy was that his boxing had improved out of this world. If he didn't get to do the *fuck and flee* portion of his routine, he was at least going to be fucking good at the *fight* part.

It also had to be said though, the lack of actual fucking in his life... that sucked.

The reason for his inability to get laid had just walked into The Roost. Violet Chapman's red hair was like a flaming beacon wherever she went, and despite being deep in a re-telling of his first fight to Dev, Tabs and Grey, he clocked her arrival almost involuntarily.

Because it wasn't like he'd been waiting for her to arrive or anything.

Fuck's sake.

He kept on talking as Violet scanned the growing crowd at The Roost. Briefly her gaze landed on him only to abruptly move away...and then snap back again.

Her eyes widened as she studied him, although Andy tried to keep his attention on Dev and not the firecracker of a woman several feet beyond.

But then Violet frowned and started walking, and didn't stop until she stood right in front of him. She put her hands on her snug, jean-clad hips.

"What have you done to yourself?" she demanded.

He casually met her glare with a nonchalant shrug. "I won a boxing tournament."

She shook her head. "That isn't worth getting your head caved in for," she sniffed with disapproval. "You're hurt."

"I won because I'm very good at not getting my head

'caved in'." He crossing his arms, starting to get irritated. This had become a pattern with all their recent conversations, this inevitable descent into an argument. "Why do you care, anyway? Just last week you told me you don't like me. I believe your words were: I've never liked you, you arrogant asshole."

That had been when he'd over-ruled her decision on a change in takeaway coffee cup supplier, and had gone over her head to cancel the order. He liked the coffee cups they already had, and had no regrets about his decision.

She sniffed again. "That still stands. But I have a responsibility to Cars & Coffee to have enough mechanics available. My latest marketing campaign means we're booked weeks ahead, Andy."

"Bullshit," he said with a wide grin, seeing the play of anger and concern in her face. "You care," he said. Crowed it, maybe, aware this had become a bit of a show, with the Shadow Team all watching on, and now Casey who'd just joined the small group. Let alone the interested gaze of the rest of The Roost's patrons. "Let the record show that Violet Chapman cares about Andy Torres."

Violet gave a little growl of protest. "No, that's not true," she said. Her gaze darted about as she seemed to realize the attention they were drawing. "Other than *purely* in the most professional sense, of course."

There was raucous, female laugh somewhere in the depths of The Roost, and then a voice sang out: "Just screw him, honey. Get it over with."

The bar went silent, and Violet sucked in a sharp breath.

Then someone laughed, someone else joined in, and a moment later Violet turned on her heel and marched out.

Andy placed his glass on the oak bar with a *thunk* before following her.

The moment Violet reached Main Street she broke into a jog. Her car was parked at a lot at the end of the alley she'd been standing in not even five minutes earlier. Five minutes earlier she'd been trying to work out why she was allowing Andy Torres – a man who didn't want her - ruin her sex life, and now she'd gone and caused a scene in front of half of Falcon?

That hadn't been the plan. The plan had been to have a drink with Casey, to finally let her friend know about all this Andy shit she'd inexplicably kept to herself, and pay *zero* attention to Andy Torres if he turned up. He wasn't even supposed to be at The Roost tonight, as she'd assumed he'd be off *fucking and fleeing* after his boxing tournament. Not standing beside the bar with a purpling bruise marring his irritatingly handsome face.

And then *her own mother* had shouted out *to the whole town* that Violet should go screw Andy.

Her cheeks burned with humiliation. She'd never seen Iris Chapman even once at The Roost, as her mother favored getting passed-out drunk in the comfort of her own home.

But she couldn't blame her humiliation on her mom. Violet had chosen to berate Andy with an audience.

Although right up until her mother spoke, it hadn't felt like that. She'd just seen his injury and something had taken over. She'd forgotten she was looking for Casey. All she'd cared about was getting to Andy. Making sure he was okay.

"Violet!"

She'd reached her Prius, and her shoulders tensed at Andy's deep voice not far behind her. She didn't look up as she tugged her car keys out of her small handbag. It was summer, so even though it was after 8pm, dusk made the sky a mess of pinks and purples. It wouldn't be fully dark for another half hour at least. The parking lot was edged with trees and dotted with vehicles, but otherwise it was deserted.

There was a *beep* as she unlocked her car, but when she reached for the door handle, Andy grabbed her wrist.

"Wait," he said.

She frowned. "Why?"

She looked down at the tanned olive skin of his large hand against her freckled paleness. Had they ever touched before? Beyond the incidental passing of a coffee cup?

She shivered, and she hated herself for that.

He doesn't want me.

"You're upset," he said.

She shrugged. "Why would *you* care? We don't like each other."

"We both know that's bullshit."

She kept staring down at his hand, focusing on the heat of his touch. "Not for me," she said stubbornly. "I don't like you at all." She swallowed, then added for good measure. "Not one little bit."

"Bullshit," he repeated. But softer this time.

Belatedly, she snatched her hand away. She turned to face him, but he was so close she ended up with her back pressed up against the Prius and Andy's tall frame towering over her. He made no move to step back to give her more space.

That should annoy her, but instead it made her pulse kick up a gear.

He doesn't want me, she told herself again.

But as she stood here in the darkening dusk, with Andy so close and her arm still tingling from his touch, that felt like a lie. But, his rejection started all of this. It started this electric, prickly dynamic. It started her year of accidental celibacy.

"I care that you're upset," he said. "Was that your mom—?"

She laughed without humor. "About the only thing I've ever been able to rely on my mom to do is embarrass me."

"I'm sorry for my part in that," he said.

She stared somewhere over his shoulder. "I don't know what came over me," she said quietly. "I caused that scene." She shook her head. "Can we just forget about it? I must be tired or something, the whole thing was just silly." She searched for a plausible reason for her behavior. "I've had a few late nights moving the Rodeo

Committee's finances to a new online accounting system. That must be it." She crossed her arms. "I just want to forget it happened."

Now she should turn and open the car door, and Andy should step back to give her space. Neither happened.

"I knew people were watching," he said, his tone gruff. "I played it up to the crowd. But I didn't want anyone to laugh at you."

"What did you want?" she asked. But her question had more meaning than she'd intended.

What did you want, Andy?

Andy cleared his throat. His gaze dropped from her eyes to her mouth before jerking back up again. "I like sparring with you," he said. "It's become a game. We both say stupid shit we don't mean."

"I did mean it that you're an idiot for refusing to try my new coffee cups." She was still being stubborn.

He raised an eyebrow as he held her gaze.

"But I didn't mean it that I've never liked you," she conceded. "That was possibly an over-reaction."

"I also never thought you were on an epic dry spell," he offered.

She blinked. "You said that months ago!" It was a morning where Torres had been piling shit on Sam for being the most eligible bachelor in Falcon – and somehow the banter had become about both her and Andy's matching long-term single-ness.

He shrugged. "I never forget a good burn," he said.

"Oh, it *was* good," Violet said with a grin, remembering the sense of triumph but not her actual words. "What did I say again?"

"You'd just assured me your dry spell was non-existent with a graphic reference to an encounter outside the Tipsy Tree in this exact back seat, I believe," he said, gesturing at her Prius. "And then you closed out with a reference to me pining after an unrequited love. My fiancée, I presume."

Her gaze dropped to his chest. "Oh dear," she said. "That wasn't very nice of me." She swallowed. "I don't really know what happened with your fiancée. I was parroting a Falcon rumor." She looked up to hold his gaze. The sun had almost set now, but there was enough light to just make out the sparks of gold in his hazel eyes. "I'm sorry. Sorry for saying it, and sorry for repeating exactly the type of Falcon gossip I hate."

"Don't sweat it," he said. "Remember I kind of just caused the whole town to laugh at you."

But that burn of humiliation had softened to barely a sting. Instead, a different heat sparked between them. "And you don't follow my stocktaking procedures correctly."

His lips quirked. "Guilty."

"Plus, you ran out of Almond milk last week."

He raised his hands in defense. "I'm the literal worst."

But he wasn't. She stood there, with Andy so close and a year of pranks and bickering... and a brutal rejection... between them.

What was this? What was happening here?

"In the bar before," she said carefully, then repeated her earlier question: "What did you want?"

Again his gaze dropped to her lips. Her belly flipped over.

But then he took a deep breath, and when his gaze met hers again it was shuttered.

"It's just like I said. I like to spar with you. It's a bit of fun, just messing around."

"Just like with the guys, right?" she pushed. "Just like with Tabs, or Grey or Dev. Right, *Torres*?"

He nodded sharply. "Exactly."

"We both know that's bullshit," she said, echoing his own words.

He blinked, then his gaze sharpened. "It's the truth."

Her laugh was dry. "Now you're the one being stubborn." She sighed. "What's going on here, Andy?"

She saw him react to her use of his first name in the tightening of his jaw. "Nothing is *going* to go on here."

She didn't miss the nuance in his words, and she was done with pretending. "Why not?" she said. "We can't go on like this."

"Like what?" he asked. "A bit of banter? What's the harm in that?"

"The harm?" She laughed, and twelve months of tension bubbled over. "Andy Torres, I haven't had sex in a year because of you, and I'm over it."

His jaw literally dropped. His gaze was now anything but shuttered.

"What did you just say?"

"Honestly, the situation is beyond ridiculous. It

would appear despite your *crystal-clear* rejection, at some level Casey was right."

"Casey?" he sounded utterly confused.

"That our prank stuff was foreplay." She shook her head. "And silly me must think all this other shit is foreplay, too, otherwise I don't know what the *fuck* I'm holding out for." Her gaze lifted to the night sky. "And I thought I didn't curse," she muttered to herself. "Fuck."

His stepped closer, crowding her against the car. "Violet," he said, sounding strangled. "I need you to say that first bit again. About the last time you had sex. Because I thought you said—"

Now she'd started, she couldn't stop. "What I'm trying to get at, Torres," she said, "is that if you don't want me, let's stop all this shit. Whether it's foreplay or you really, truly believe I'm one of the guys and couldn't give a shit if I had a cock or clit under my jeans—"

"Jesus H. Christ," he managed between gritted teeth. "Violet—"

"It *has* to stop. Do you get it? *Finito. Done.* Because honestly, I really don't want you living rent free in my head when some other guy is trying to get into my pants."

"*What other guy, Violet?*"

"That's not the point, Torres," she said, frowning as she looked up at him. The fading light caused dramatic shadows beneath his brow and cheekbones.

"I can assure you it's *entirely* the point."

She threw her hands up in exasperation, but he was so close her fingertips brushed briefly against his chest. She swallowed a gasp at the intensity of her body's response from that simple, accidental touch. "You do not get to go all caveman, Torres. You don't get to give a shit about men who *actually* want me, when you don't."

His gaze flicked to the sky as he swallowed. He was so close she could feel the tension vibrating from his body.

"It's just a bit of silly banter," he said between gritted teeth, still staring somewhere above her head. He swallowed again, then caught her gaze. "That's all. That's all."

But it felt like he was saying the words to himself, not to her. And the lie they were was evident in everything about this moment. In his utterly unnecessary but delicious proximity, in the heat in his gaze, and in the harshness of the deep breaths he took as he stared at her.

He was lying to himself, and to her. But had she always known this? Had that been their game all this time?

But she was sick and tired of stupid games.

"Torres," she said firmly. "Just so we're clear. You don't want me. You *don't get to care* about the guy I could go pick up at the Tipsy Tree tonight, right?" Her words were husky. "You don't get to care if he kisses me and makes me hot." She swallowed, not even shocked by her boldness. She *had* to push. She *had* to know. "You don't get to care if he lays me down on the back seat of his truck, unbuttons my blouse and takes off the hot-as-hell lacy bra I thought of *you* when I bought."

"*Violet*—" Her name was a groan and a plea.

But she didn't stop as her words dropped down to a

whisper. "You don't get to care when I unsnap my jeans for him. When I—"

She went abruptly silent as he pressed a hand across her mouth. Then pushed his body against hers. Hard. She was shoved up against her car and he was so damn immovable against her, his hand not gentle against her lips, pressing against her teeth.

Her eyes widened in something that maybe should've been fear given his superior size and the fire in his gaze.

But she wasn't scared.

She'd never been so turned on in her life, and as he deliberately rubbed his erection against her belly, her thighs clenched and she could feel the slickness of her panties.

With a groan his head fell forward as he nuzzled her neck, his hand not moving from her lips.

"You bought lingerie for me," he grunted against her skin, his breath hot. It was a statement, not a question, yet she nodded. "You let other men touch you when you're thinking of *me*," he said. He nipped the sensitive skin beneath her ear and she shivered. "Don't do that again. No one touches you but me." His other hand crept between their bodies to curl inside the front waist band of her jeans. He tugged her upwards and against him, drag ging the seam of her jeans hard against her clit. She gasped.

"But Torres—" she mumbled against his fingers.

"*Andy*," he demanded roughly against her ear. "Call me Andy."

"Andy..."

His name was muffled against his palm but he rewarded her with a hot kiss against her neck, and the thrust of his cock against the front of her jeans. She moaned.

"Mine," he said, then nipped her again, like a brand. "All fucking mine."

She undulated against his cock desperately.

"You knew, smart girl, all along," he said against her neck. "You knew what you did to me. Knew what I wanted to do to you."

"*Yes...*"

She reached blindly upwards to pull his hand away from her lips so she could kiss him. She was so desperate to taste him. Desperate to touch him everywhere. Desperate for *him.*

But as her fingers grasped his wrist and tugged, he went still.

Then he straightened, and his expression was one of horror as he looked down at her plastered between his body and the car, his hand still firm against her mouth, his fingers still hooked inside her jeans as he held her so effortlessly against his cock.

"What the fuck am I doing?" he said harshly, shaking his head. "What the actual fuck..."

He stepped back, but caught her around the waist when she sagged against the car door.

"Are you okay, Violet?" he said urgently. "Did I hurt you?"

Still hazy with lust and heat, she reached for him. "Don't stop," she sighed.

But he shook his head again. "I'm a damn animal," he muttered to himself. "No control. No fucking control..."

His gaze flicked over her as he appeared to assess her stability before dropping his hands from her waist.

With the absence of his touch, she shivered.

"*This* is why this shouldn't happen. Why it can't happen," he muttered, frowning. Then he caught her gaze again. "Do you get it now?" he said, his words stark in the deserted parking lot she was only now, once again, aware of.

"Get what?"

Yet another shake of his head. "I am so sorry, Violet."

Something shifted in his gaze. The shutters were back.

She wanted to scream with frustration.

"I *liked* that," she said. "*All of it.*"

But he wasn't listening. "I could've hurt you."

"No," she said firmly.

But she knew she'd lost him. The wildness had gone, replaced with the man who she only now realized so very tightly held himself in check.

"Violence is for the boxing ring," he said roughly.

She laughed in shock. "That wasn't violent. It was hot."

"I've never lost it so completely like that," he said, but again to himself. She hated this. Hated how he was closing himself off from her. "I'd hoped I was different, but knew I wasn't, and I was right."

She had to lean close to catch his muttered words.

"Different to who?"

"It doesn't matter," he said. He was looking at her but avoiding her gaze.

"Yes, it does—"

But he cut her off. "I'm sorry," he said. "I have to go."

"Pardon me?"

But he'd already backed several steps further away, back towards The Roost.

"I'm sorry," he said again. "Forget this ever happened." His gaze snapped up and down her body dismissively. "I have."

"*What?*" she swallowed. "Don't be stupid Andy. I don't know what you're concerned about, but you just said *I was yours*. You can't walk away now with no explanation."

He looked at her properly. For long, long seconds. He continued to hold her gaze as he spoke. "I was caught up in the moment," he said coolly. "I didn't mean it."

Suddenly she was cold. Suddenly she felt dangerously like she had nine months earlier, but this time it wasn't Andy naked, it was her. Stripped naked and vulnerable with her honesty. She'd stupidly told him everything.

She was so, so damn stupid.

The brutality of his rejection was a stab and a twist to her chest.

"You were leaving," she said in clipped tones as he lingered.

"I'm sorry—"

"*Don't*," she said.

He left.

She watched him walk away, then turned and took a deep breath as she gripped the car door handle. Her shoulders prickled with the sense of being watched.

Had he stopped? Had he changed his mind?

She laughed dryly.

No. She had more pride than that.

She climbed into her car and drove home. She didn't look back.

SEVEN

VIOLET ARRIVED HOME TO FIND HER GRANDMOTHER asleep on her floral-printed couch, her beloved Colin Firth version of *Pride & Prejudice* blaring on the screen thanks to her nanna's stubborn refusal to wear her hearing aids.

She left Elizabeth Bennet to endure Mr Collins' company at Rosings Park as she gently woke her Nanna and took her upstairs to her room. A few minutes later she paused before turning off the DVD as she realized she was watching Darcy's ill-fated first proposal.

"...you chose to tell me that you like me against your will, against your reason..."

The context was utterly different, yet Elizabeth's angry words to Darcy echoed in Violet's head after the TV screen had gone black. In the kitchen she made herself a hot chocolate, then sat at the breakfast bar and didn't drink it. Instead, she squeezed her eyes tight shut.

Twice she'd let Andy Torres reject her. Yet here she

was attempting to work out the *why*. Trying to convince herself there was more to what had just happened than electric physical attraction. That what Andy had said had *meant* something: *You're mine.*

In the moment, she'd believed him.

And even now she was foolishly casting herself as Lizzie Bennett and Andy as Mr Darcy, and that his rejection was somehow against his will, and against what he wanted.

Ha! She was an idiot.

Clearly Andy had something going on, with his talk of violence and being different. Even now she itched to make that giant of a man *tell her* what the heck had freaked him out so much.

But he'd chosen to be cruel in his rejection. He'd chosen – twice now – to hurt her rather than explain. The first time maybe that'd been understandable – they'd hardly known each other. But this time...

There was a sound behind her, outside.

Violet swiveled on her bar stool. It hadn't been anything loud – more a soft thud. There was a tiny circular dining table between her and the glass sliding door that led out to her Nanna's porch. She hadn't drawn the drapes, but with the lights on inside all Violet could see in the darkness was her own reflection. She slid off the chair and around the table to switch on the porch-light, wondering if Gus the curious labradoodle had once again escaped from the neighbors. But nothing was revealed by the porchlight other than her Nanna's new cast iron bird-bath and an empty yard.

A squirrel, maybe?

Violet carried her hot chocolate into the lounge, kicked off her heels and restarted Pride & Prejudice. She needed something to distract herself from the galling realization that despite everything – she still wished Andy had kissed her before his second humiliating rejection. How goddamn pathetic was that?

She'd left her phone on the coffee table and ignored a message notification from Andy in favor of watching Mr Darcy drag himself out of the lake at Pemberley. His message remained unread when she went searching for an emergency block of chocolate at the back of the fridge.

Surely between Colin Firth and the healing properties of Hershey's, tonight wouldn't be a total bust?

Chocolate in hand, she closed the stainless-steel fridge door.

A shadow moved in the door's dull reflection.

"Nanna?" she asked as she went to turn around.

But it was not her grandmother behind her.

A hand smothered her scream as strong arms wrapped around her and lifted her from the ground. For the second time tonight fingers covered her lips, but this man definitely wasn't Andy. His fingers pressed painfully against her teeth and tasted of sweat and something stale. She kicked and squirmed in panic and desperation, trying to bite and scream but unable to open her mouth against the brutal grip on her lips. She landed a blow to the man's shin and he swore. Then *another* man stepped in front of her.

She screamed uselessly again. *What the hell was going on?*

Why the fuck were these men in her grandmother's house?

Icy fear for her helpless Nanna sleeping upstairs temporarily paused her struggle.

"Good girl," the man in front of her said softly. He was dressed all in black, a hoodie drawn low over his forehead throwing his face in shadow. There was a *snick* as the man flicked open a horrifically sharp blade.

She screamed again. Kicked again.

The man calmly gestured back towards the lounge. "Want me to go upstairs?" he asked in an impossibly calm tone.

She fought even harder as she screamed a *no* the man couldn't hear.

"Stop fighting," the man said. "Make this easy for us and I don't bother the little old lady upstairs." He shrugged. "Make this hard and I slit her throat."

She could taste her own tears amongst the brute's sweaty fingers. Her stomach roiled.

But she remained still.

"Good girl," the man said again, stretching his fleshy lips into a smile.

She mumbled unintelligible questions against the hand against her lips: *Who are you? Make what hard?*

But they didn't bother to understand her, instead the man in the hoodie flicked closed his blade before fishing a fistful of zip ties out of his pocket.

Violet shuddered as she allowed the man to tie her

ankles together, her mind racing. *How could she just allow this? Was she making it even easier for these men to hurt Nanna by not fighting? Was she being kidnapped? Why on earth hadn't she ever asked the special forces soldiers she worked with to teach her self-defense?*

After her wrists were tied in front of her, the man met her gaze, close enough she could smell tuna on his breath. His dull blue eyes were bloodshot.

"We're just going to borrow you for a little while, Miss Chapman, then we'll return you right back," he said.

He knew her name? Borrow her?

"And I *know* you'll be well behaved," the man continued, grabbing a black cloth from the back pocket of his jeans. "Otherwise, I'll make a trip upstairs when we return. Got it?"

She was being held so firm she could barely move her head, but she attempted a nod. What other choice did she have?

The man in the hoodie rolled the cloth into a strip, then shoved it into her mouth the instant the brute behind her dropped his hand. A moment later the gag was knotted at the back of her head and she was being carried outside like a baby. Across the patio in the darkness. Past the birdbath.

Her Nanna's lot backed onto parkland, and the man who carried her tossed her over his shoulder before opening the gate in the picket fence. Her heart raced as she breathed rapidly through her nose and blood rushed to her head.

What do I do? What do I do?

"We've got a visitor," the brute grunted a moment before a car's headlights momentarily illuminated the backyard. Someone had parked in her Nanna's driveway.

The lights switched off.

"I'll go sort it," hoodie man said. "Take her to the van and meet me out front."

Sort it?

Who was it?

Andy? He'd messaged her. Had he come over to... apologize? Explain?

Or was it Casey coming to check on her?

No. No.

She couldn't let either of them be hurt. She couldn't just do nothing. A sudden, desperate wiggle dislodged her from the man's shoulder and she hit the lawn hard. But when she tried to stand, she remembered too late how she'd so stupidly allowed the men to bind her wrists and ankles. Still, she struggled to get to her feet, her fingers desperate and useless as they pushed impotently against the dirt and grass.

Then something – a boot – slammed into her gut. She curled into a ball as pain radiated from her belly and blurred her vision. Then she was wrenched upwards and over the man's shoulder once again.

"Next time I won't be so gentle," he grunted as he strode through the gate.

In the parkland the darkness was absolute.

And as she hung upside down her tears of pain and fear soaked into the fabric of her captor's shirt.

. . .

He'd been an asshole.

Such a fucking asshole.

The moment Andy returned to The Roost he'd known he'd fucked up. Yep, he'd managed to convince himself his behavior had been *necessary* as he'd walked away from Violet. He still had no doubt he'd been right to stop their... embrace.

Was that what he was going to call it?

Jesus Christ.

He bumped his forehead against his steering wheel as he sat parked in Violet's driveway. Jesus *Fucking* Christ. That had been no "embrace". It had been the single hottest moment of his life, and he hadn't even kissed her mouth.

Nope, instead he'd held her against the car and shoved his hand across her mouth like a goddamn animal. Stopping *that* had been correct. But what he'd said after...

That was why he was here.

Sitting in his truck trying to work out what to say was clearly ineffective, so he got out and jogged the short distance to the front porch. His boots thumped up the wooden steps, and triggered the porch light to switch on. Light also glowed beyond the closed drapes of the downstairs rooms, and he could hear something playing on the TV.

He rapped sharply on the front door, then cringed as he remembered how early his own grandmother – his Avó - used to go to bed. He couldn't hear any movement inside. Should he call Violet's cell? Or was she simply ignoring him?

Likely.

He could easily summon an image of Violet frowning angrily at her front door, as he'd become incredibly adept at frustrating the fiery, clever red-head over the past several months. Her brows would draw just slightly together and she'd scrunch her nose as her emerald green eyes would darken with infuriated intensity.

The image made him smile as he reaching into his pocket for his cell. And now he also knew how she looked when her incredible eyes were dark with heat and passion. He knew the vanilla scent of her skin and the way she shivered when he-

Something struck him in the back of the head.

In the split second he remained conscious before his head smacked against the porch floor, he glimpsed a man dressed in black, rock in hand. A man Andy was taller than, and bigger than. A man he should've heard coming, who he should've taken down in moments.

But he'd done neither of those things.

Was this man here to hurt Violet?

No. No. No.

He hit the ground and everything went black.

EIGHT

SHE WAS THROWN ONTO THE BACK ROW OF SEATS. The brute wasn't careful with her, and with her hands tied at her front she couldn't prevent her forehead banging against the wall of the van. Dazed and in pain, she lay still as her vision slid back into somewhat focus. Her glasses were long gone and she had no idea when they'd fallen off.

Her tears had stopped, but her heart continued to gallop at speed.

Why was this happening?

Had the other man hurt Andy? Or Casey?

The van door was yanked opened and something was manhandled in by the two men. Where she lay and with another row of seats in front of her, she couldn't properly see what they were doing, but when the object was finally dropped with a *thud* to the van floor, a boot dropped into her view.

Andy!

"What's your plan here, boss?" the brute asked. "Guy's still breathing."

"We'll dump him somewhere on the way," the smaller man replied easily.

She tried to gasp, but just ended up coughing and choking on her gag.

Hoodie guy – the boss, she supposed – turned to her. Without her glasses and in the darkness, both men were near featureless, not that she needed anything to make this situation more terrifying.

"Worried about your boyfriend, lady?" the boss asked. Then he laughed. "Enjoyed the show in the parking lot before, gotta say. Dude's an idiot to walk away from what you were throwing at him."

These two men were *watching* her before?

Was it their eyes she'd felt on her back after Andy walked away?

Why? Why watch her then? Why take her now?

She shook her head in an attempt to steady her thoughts as the men slammed the door shut again.

They'd said Andy was still breathing. He was alive.

He's alive. He's alive. He's alive.

She wiggled until she was sitting up, then as the two men climbed into the front of the van, she quickly lay down again so they wouldn't notice her change of position. Now her head was near Andy's boots, and as she lay there she cursed her poor eyesight. She could see his boots clear as day, but from his knees and beyond, Andy was infuriatingly blurry. She could see the rise and fall of his chest as he breathed. But she couldn't tell if his eyes were open. Was he unconscious?

She thought so. His stillness was too absolute.

What had they done to him?

The van started up and began to move. There were no windows in the back part but the glow of streetlights regularly flooded the front seat as the van weaved its way out of Falcon.

Where were they taking her?

And why?

She twisted her wrists in their ties. She was barefoot, the ties at her ankles digging into her skin. Her favorite green heels were in her lounge with Pride & Prejudice still playing. Violet's throat tightened as she imagined her Nanna's horror when she discovered her missing.

Maybe I'll be back before she wakes up?

Wasn't that what the man said, the boss? *We're just going to borrow you for a little while, Miss Chapman.*

Had they really meant that? Would they really allow her to see their faces but still return her safe and well? It seemed an impossibility.

She could feel tears well up again, but she swallowed them back. She had no chance at all if she panicked. She was a smart person, she had to *think*. She had to stay calm.

She *had* to make it home.

And she *had* to make sure Andy made it home safely too.

She studied his large form as she took deep breath after deep breath, remembering how she'd been taught how to breathe in squares at some corporate professional development day in New York.

Exhale...two...three...four

Inhale...two...three...four

Hold my breath...two...three...four...

She doubted the facilitator ever expected her technique would be used during a kidnapping – but Violet had to admit it was helping.

She was still absolutely terrified. But her brain now felt less like a runaway train.

Andy had big feet. That was the first thing she focused on. It was too dark in the back of the van for the color of his jeans to be obvious, but she knew they were a charcoal grey as she'd definitely noticed in The Roost. She always noticed pretty much everything about Andy. He'd pulled on his battered brown leather jacket before coming to her place, and she could see his navy-blue t-shirt beneath it. Sprawled like he was, it seemed impossible that someone so large could be so vulnerable. But right now, unconscious, he was even *more* vulnerable than she was, and she felt her stomach lurch at the idea that Andy – a man she'd always felt had an aura of invincibility – could be in danger.

What were these two men going to do to Andy?

As she stared at Andy her stubborn refusal to accept how she felt about this man felt impossibly immature. Yes, she had wanted him. But the why... the why she'd pushed aside until now. Because if all she'd wanted was a tall, ripped retired special forces soldier then Andy was not the only option at Cars & Coffee. In fact, one night at

The Roost Caleb had come right out and propositioned her in his easy, lackadaisical way. He'd been clear about what he was interested in: her body, so they could scratch a shared itch. And when she'd declined his offer his easy acceptance of her refusal had been both refreshing and almost a little insulting. He hadn't been bothered at all – there had been no emotion behind his invitation. Yet *every single* interaction with Andy had been saturated in... emotion. No – that didn't cover it.

Passion. Both passionate fury and just plain old passion. Every single time.

"Torres is a moron," Caleb had said at the time, and when she'd vehemently replied:

"What has Torres got to do with it?"

Caleb had just laughed as she'd bristled.

But Andy had everything to do with it. Because this wasn't just about sex and about attraction. Or about passion, even.

She liked him. She really liked Andy. She liked his easy banter with every customer who visited his coffee van. She liked his willingness to pitch in in the garage whenever needed. She liked how kind he was to Casey's daughters when they visited. She liked how randomly he'd curse in Portuguese, and that one time he brought brigadeiros – fudge balls – into Cars & Coffee to share with everyone in honor of his late Brazilian grandmother's birthday. She admired - although he never spoke of it - his former career in the Special Forces, and the drive and commitment that would've been required to become a Delta Force operator. And she liked that no matter how barbed their banter had become, he *always* brought her a morning almond milk latte.

She wanted to know so much more about him.

More than the taste of his mouth or the feel of his body.

She wanted to know what demons shuttered his gaze. What had caused the fear and horror in his expression when he'd realized he'd been somewhat manhandling her against her Prius.

She wanted to know everything there was to know about Andy Torres, and she wanted him to know everything there was to know about her.

Andy might not want any of that. In fact, all evidence so far pointed to a reality that he absolutely did *not*. But that didn't matter right now. Right now she had this extraordinary man stuck with her in this awful situation and she couldn't entertain the possibility that he wouldn't be okay. *She could not.*

Had he moved?

She fought to make her eyes focus, but he remained infuriatingly blurry. But… maybe. She thought maybe he'd shifted his head slightly. Was he waking up?

What could she do?

She needed to be able to talk to him. At the front of the van the men had the radio going, some late-night talk show with awkward listener questions.

Her hands were zip tied to her front, so she lifted them, attempting to hook her fingers into her painful gag – feeling extremely stupid for not trying this earlier. The fabric was so tight she could barely shift it, but through pushing with her tongue and her fingers she managed to move it upwards, until only her top lip was covered by the gag.

"Andy?" she whispered.

He groaned and rocked a little on the floor. His hands were tied behind his back, but his feet were untied.

That was good, right? Violet didn't know the specifics of what Delta Force Operators could do, but she had zero doubt Andy was a thousand times more skilled than the men who'd kidnapped her. If she could get his wrists untied, could he overpower them?

She was certain the answer was yes.

But she needed him lucid, and his hands free.

How?

She glanced to the front of the van. Neither man had looked back once, apparently confident she was compliant and Andy was no threat.

The van bumped over an undulation in the road, dislodging her from her seat. She tumbled onto the floor with a thud, followed by a laugh from the front of the van.

The boss of the pair looked back at her, temporarily lit up by a convenient street lamp.

"Careful back there!" he guffawed. "Need to keep you in one piece."

For what?

The man turned back to the road leaving Violet on the floor, immediately behind Andy's boots. *This was good.*

She shuffled upwards, ignoring the aches and twinges

in her body that this latest fall amplified. On her knees, she pushed Andy's lower legs to the right to give her more space. That took a few goes, his legs surprisingly heavy.

Through all this, Andy barely moved. He still breathed slow and steady, but no more groans or movement. She repeatedly glanced to the front of the van, but her captors never looked back.

She shuffled forward again until her knees rested against his butt. She reached with her tied hands for his wrists, quickly realizing his hands were also zip-tied together. *Fuck.* She gripped his hands – still warm and strong – as she leaned forward over his prone body to whisper in his ear.

"Andy?" she said.

His body was much longer than hers and with her hands tied she needed to lay clumsily against him. Even unconscious, his size and heat was reassuring.

"Please wake up Andy," she tried again. "Please. Andy." She swallowed, then tried again in a whispered version of the tone she'd used when he'd canceled her coffee cup order. "I need you to wake up *now*, Torres. Right this instant, you understand me?"

He gave another low moan but didn't move.

She squeezed his hands as she pushed against his shoulders with her body, trying to shake him awake. "Andy...*please*."

They drove beneath another street lamp, and momentarily the van was flooded with light. In that moment she realized Andy was... *smiling*? His eyes were shut, but that was definitely a grin.

"What the hell, Torres!" she whispered urgently. "This isn't a joke. You aren't dreaming. This is real. You *have* to wake up."

"Feels..." he said, so low and husky she could barely hear it. "...feels like a dream. To have you..." He frowned. "Why does my head hurt?"

For the first time she noticed the blood that matted the back of his head. "Someone hit you," she said. Hatred for the man who'd hurt Andy flooded her body. She glanced to the front of the van again. No one was watching them. "I'll explain later."

"Later..." he said. "After we have sex?"

"*What?*"

"Isn't that why we're in bed together?" he asked, his words confused. "I know we haven't had sex yet, as I'd *know*. Fuck, Violet, I don't know how I let this happen but I'm too fucking weak to push you out of my bed." He chuckled. "I mean mentally weak when it comes to you, but goddamn my body feels fucking useless too. What the hell is going on?"

"Someone kidnap—"

"Say you're at least naked, Vi," he interrupted, "say I've at least got that bit right... *Wait*. What did you say?"

Andy's words were slow and dazed as he regained consciousness.

"We're not in your bed, Andy," she said. "We're in a van."

The van had begun to slow, and all that panic she'd successfully shoved aside returned with a vengeance.

"And I need you to wake up properly, Andy," she said urgently. "I need your help."

But the van had come to a stop.

Her heart hammered against her chest.

The door was yanked upon. She was too late.

Andy loosely gripped her fingers as the two men came into view, but he was still confused and groggy. He shook his head as if trying to clear it of its fog.

"Oh, isn't this sweet!" said the ringleader. "The lovers are having one last cuddle."

Then without warning he grabbed Andy's legs. The brute grabbed his shoulders.

And just like that he was wrenched from her grasp. She screamed as Andy was taken from her. And then she screamed again as she realized they were parked on a bridge, and she could hear the sound of rushing water – the Colorado River.

She flung herself forward, rolling herself from the van and onto the asphalt.

"You going to try and stop us, lady?" the man holding Andy's boots asked. He paused, then dropped Andy's legs abruptly before striding over to where Violet lay. As she tried to clamber to her feet he scooped her up and threw her back into the van. She hit the edge of a row of seats and fell to the carpeted floor, winded.

Then he slammed the van door.

"Let's do this and get the fuck out of here." The boss's voice was muffled through the walls of the van.

Frantic, Violet gasped for air even as she tried uselessly to get to her feet.

She had to get up. She had to get up.

But moments later the men had returned to the van. They didn't say a word as they opened the doors and clambered back into the seats, or as the vehicle started up and drove away.

A minute later the boss twisted around to yell at her.

"Shut up, you silly bitch. All that noise isn't gonna make your boyfriend float."

And only then did she realize she was sobbing.

NINE

It'd been such a nice dream.

Andy had been in bed with Violet Chapman.

She'd been curled, naked, against his back as she'd murmured softly in his ear.

He'd had dreams like this before. *Many* dreams like this before.

A metric shit-ton if he was honest.

Although, to be fair, his previous dreams had been more graphic. Less urgent whispering in his ear, and more urgent fu-

He came fully awake as he hit the water.

Brutally, suddenly, absolutely awake.

He sunk like a stone, bumping hard against a boulder as water shoved him along.

Was he in a river?

The current pulled him deeper, and in the darkness he fought back panic as he realized he couldn't work out which direction to kick towards to reach the surface.

He let the river lead the way as he forced himself to be still as he assessed what the hell was going on.

Why the fuck am I in a river? Why are my hands tied?

His feet hit the ground and he pushed as hard as he could directly upwards, kicking strongly until he burst through the endless water to reach the surface, gasping for much needed air.

Oxygen brought with it sudden clarity.

Violet's house. A man with a rock.

Being dragged from a black van.

Violet screaming despite a gag around her lips.

Violet.

Absolute horror flooded his body as he comprehended that Violet was still in that van. Tied up and helpless with at least two violent men.

Oh, fuck...*Violet.*

He took several huge shuddering breaths as he fought back useless panic. He could *not* waste time losing his shit. Violet needed him to channel the rigid calm that'd served him well his whole damn career.

Pull yourself the fuck together, Torres.

He shouted the words into the darkness, then focused on his surroundings and making a goddamn plan.

In the moonlight he could make out three large concrete bridges arranged close together. He'd been flung from a bridge on the interstate, somewhere in the middle of nowhere as not one streetlamp lit the highway. The water was calmer now he was some distance from the bridges and he was able to kick to the edge of the river without much difficulty despite his tied wrists. On the river's edge he remained on his side as he maneuvered his tied hands under his butt and stood as he carefully stepped one leg, then the other, into the circle of his tied hands. Arms now at his front he assessed the strength of the zip ties before using his teeth to move the lock until it was directly between his wrists and the tie was pressed against his forearms. Another tug of the tie tightened it enough to remove the small slack in the tie, then he simply lifted his arms up, then down and apart – *hard.*

The ties snapped easily.

He immediately reached into his pocket for his cell, but only confirmed what he already knew – his phone wasn't there. He had the faintest memory of glimpsing it beneath the van's seats as he was dragged away from Violet.

Fuck.

He clambered up the slope away from the river, negotiating shrubs and large stones along the way. Once the land became flat he broke into a run, heading for the interstate. Even in darkness the mountains that flanked the highway were obvious, reaching high towards the stars. He was certain he hadn't been unconscious long, and that he was definitely still in Colorado. But where, he had no idea.

However, his location was of far lesser importance than Violet's.

Who were those fuckers?

Where had they taken her?

He needed to call Shadow Operations. He needed

every bit of tech and intel Shadow Ops had to find Violet *now*.

Back at the bridge, Andy surveyed the landscape. There wasn't a single street lamp as far as he could see in either direction. But maybe half a mile away he could see light. A house? A shop?

Didn't matter. Once again, he ran.

VIOLET QUIETENED HER SOBS, not wanting the assholes who'd hurt Andy to witness the depth of her pain.

Who'd hurt him?

Or... killed him?

She didn't know how long she cried, her whole body shaking with grief as the patch of wet tears on the carpeted floor grew and grew.

Maybe he woke up. Maybe the bridge wasn't that high. Maybe he's alive.

In the end, that hope was enough to slow her tears: *maybe he's alive.*

She had to hang onto that or she would completely unravel.

She curled up into a tiny ball on the floor as the van continued its journey.

As the miles passed, her grief transitioned into anger. As she listened to her captor's inane conversations, her hatred grew. How *dare* these men hurt Andy. How *dare* they kidnap her.

She needed to pull herself together, *escape*, then go back to that bridge and find Andy.

Yes.

That's what she needed to do.

The van slowed and started to bump along the road – a stark contrast to the smooth asphalt of the interstate. She slid backwards towards the rear row of seats due to a slight incline. They were heading higher into the mountains.

Her wrists bumped against the metal feet that attached the rear row of seats to the van's floor. She explored the shape of the metal with her fingers. It wasn't sharp, but maybe if she rubbed her zip-tie handcuffs against it for long enough, it might weaken the straps?

Maybe it was a dumb idea, but Violet didn't care.

She was going to give it a try.

THE LAVA BAR & Grill appeared to be mostly bar and not much grill, judging by Andy's first impressions when he opened the door with a squeal of its rusty hinges. There wasn't a single table, but there was a long bar made of rough sawn oak and clad with corrugated metal sheets. On the wall behind the bar Coors and Corona advertising flanked an impressive pair of moose antlers, while a football game played above the head of a barman who looked barely old enough to drink. None of the four men seated at the bar appeared to notice his arrival, but the youthful barman's eyes widened.

Andy strode to the bar, his soaked boots leaving wet footprints on the plank flooring.

"I need to use your phone."

The barman's gaze flicked over him, taking in his wet, plastered-on clothing and damp hair. "Are you okay?"

Andy's nod was impatient. "I need to make a phone call *right now*." The barman frowned. "Please," Andy added. "A woman is in danger."

"From you?" a slurred voice at the bar asked.

Andy pivoted to face the craggy, weathered face of a grey-haired man wearing a Broncos hoodie.

"No," Andy said firmly. Then dismissed the man to focus on the barman. "Phone, *please*?"

But the barman's gaze flicked to Broncos hoodie.

"Seems to me," Broncos slurred, "that *yooooun*, could be the danger."

"I'm not." Again, he looked to the bar man.

"You sure? Absoluuuuuutely sure?" Broncos laughed unevenly. "You seem the type."

"*What type's that?*"

It was a moment later Andy realized the bar had gone completely still, and all eyes were on him – with his fingers curled into that damn Denver Broncos hoodie, and the old man yanked out of his seat and dragged close to his clenched jaw.

The man had gone white as a sheet beneath the bar's fluorescent lighting.

"I'm sorry!" the man spluttered. "I didn't mean anything by it."

Broncos hoodie was absolutely terrified. *Of him.*

Andy released him abruptly. "*Fuck.* I'm sorry," he said. "But I *need* to make this phone call." He turned back to the barman. "Please."

The barman shifted his weight uneasily. Broncos staggered back towards his seat, his gaze wary.

Andy dragged a frustrated hand through his soaked hair, and discovered his head was bleeding when every set of eyes in the place stared at the blood he'd smeared all over his hand.

Panic made him want to leap over the bar and grab the cordless phone he could see on the counter beneath the moose antlers. Or grab Broncos again and demand he hand over his cell.

Where was Violet? What were those men doing to Violet?

Every second counted.

"Make the call for me, then," he said, holding the barman's gaze. "I know I look feral. A stranger hit me with a rock and threw me in the Colorado river, and kidnapped a woman I care about. I promise you *I* am not the threat. To her, or to you."

His words made absolutely no difference to the uneasy atmosphere. No one moved. The cold of the river felt like it had seeped into his bones. The football commentators on the TV screen were earnestly breaking down a replay of who the hell knew what.

"Call the sheriff, then. The police. Whoever you want."

His voice shook with the effort to remain calm.

The barman moved, and Andy shook his head as he realized what the kid was doing. There was a clunk as a handgun was laid onto the countertop.

"We don't want any trouble here," the barman said,

his words a little high pitched. "I think it's best you moved on."

Andy raised both his hands in a gesture of surrender. "Dude, *please*. A woman I..."

...care about?

That didn't come close to describing how he felt about Violet. But as he struggled for the right words his gaze landed on his wrist. An idea formed.

"Let's start again," Andy said. "I propose a simple transaction. This watch, for the loan of your cell." He nodded at his wrist. "Look it up. It's a Tag Heuer Autavia. Yours to keep, if you just let me borrow your phone."

The barman frowned and glanced at the captive audience at the bar.

One already had his phone out. He was totally bald and his scalp shone with sweat. His eyes widened a few moments later. "Who the heck pays that much for a watch?" the man asked.

Andy shrugged. "I like watches," he said. He quickly undid the watch and tossed it at the barman. "Check it out. It's real."

The kid caught the heavy, black tactical watch and turned it over in his hands before leaning over to confer with the bald guy.

Every fucking second counts.

His jaw was so tense his head pounded.

Finally, the barman nodded. He fished his phone out of his back pocket and tossed it at Andy. Andy caught it easily. The screen was cracked and it was years old – but it was fully charged.

"Doesn't have a passcode," the barman said, now ignoring Andy. In fact, everyone was ignoring Andy as they gathered around his watch.

So much for their concern.

Phone gripped hard, Andy opened the browser to search for The Roost's phone number. As he'd sprinted to this dive of a bar, he'd realized he didn't have one single useful number memorized. He didn't have the number for Shadow Ops, or for any member of the Shadow Team. But The Roost would still be open.

Even if the Shadow Team had left, *someone* there would be able to find them.

He made the call.

It rang out. He called again, trying to remain calm.

He'd been in damn warzones, he'd survived a fucking hotel siege – and *now* he was terrified?

Someone picked up.

"Is Sam Taberner there?" he demanded. Loud music blasted in the background.

"You'll have to speak up!" a female voice laughed over the phone. "It's going off in here!"

He tried again. "Is Sam Taberner there? Or Caleb Grey? Dev McCarthy?"

It was late, and it was unlikely any of the Shadow Team was still at The Roost, but really all he needed was someone who could contact any one of them.

Another laugh that could barely be heard over the ruckus.

"Sorry can't hear a thing! Call back tomorrow."

She'd hung up. Andy stared at the phone in disbelief.

He rang back. No one answered.

He swore viciously as he googled the number for Cars & Coffee, on the very off chance someone was there. There wasn't.

None of the Shadow Team were on social media – it was the antithesis of the covert work they did. Instead, all their communication was via secure cell phones or a secure messaging app – which was all well and good unless you *fucking lost your phone.*

"What's your number?" he barked at the barman. The barman wore Andy's watch on his skinny wrist as he poured a beer, but he paused mid pour before snatching up a pen and a soggy coaster. Andy grabbed the coaster once the number had been scribbled down and logged into his email account via the phone browser. He couldn't log into the secure email he used for Shadow Team comms, but he could log into the Gmail account he'd had forever. He shot off the briefest email to Sam, Dev and Caleb with his new number in the subject line, then turned to the men at the bar.

"Who wants to sell me their car?"

TEN

Finally the van came to a stop.

They'd left anything resembling a smooth road what felt like hours ago. Although Violet found it difficult to judge the passing of time while being haphazardly tossed about in the back of a van. She'd long ago given up trying to saw through her zip ties. Instead, she'd braced herself between the door and a row of seats as she'd attempted to minimize the distance she bounced with every pothole or rut.

Everything hurt. She'd been kicked, dropped, thrown and jostled over the past several hours, and her whole body ached. She had a headache from crying and her useless attempts to focus on her surroundings without her glasses.

The men had gotten out of the van and she heard the crunch of their boots on gravel and the murmur of their voices as they walked away.

As long minutes passed and her fear at what might

come next grew, she no longer felt grateful the van had stopped.

Now what?

What was going to happen to her now?

At the sound of returning footsteps, her heart-rate accelerated once again. She was so utterly helpless with her wrists and ankles still tied firm and her poor eyesight. Her internal bravado of before seemed laughable now. Escape and go get Andy?

How the hell was she going to do that?

She flinched as the van door was yanked open. Outside it was still dark, although beyond the man who stood over her she could see a well-lit wooden cabin.

It was the bigger man who'd opened the van door. He didn't speak as he grabbed her bare foot to drag her closer to the door and then picked her up with as much care as if she were a sack of potatoes.

"Where are we?" she asked as she dangled over his shoulder, but the man didn't respond.

In her blouse and jeans and with bare feet, the air was cool. She shivered.

He opened the door to the cabin, where it was equally cold, then dumped her onto a lumpy, floral-print couch. A moment after he dropped her, something landed on her chest.

Her glasses. They had sky-blue acetate frames a few shades lighter than her navy-blue satin blouse.

"Oh!" she exclaimed, awkwardly attempting to grab them with her bound hands.

She cringed as the brute's fingers brushed her breasts as he picked her glasses up. "You'll need these," he said.

"No touching," cautioned the smaller man. He had his back to them both as he leaned over a wooden dining table. He sounded bored as he continued. "You know our instructions."

The brute rolled his eyes as he flicked open her glasses and slid them onto her nose. It was the first time she'd seen this man clearly. He had ruddy skin and a bulbous nose with enormous pores.

He met her gaze with his muddy brown eyes as he roughly undid her gag before stepping back. "Later," he said, with a twist of his lips.

Violet swallowed the bile that lurched in her throat.

"Laptop's dead," muttered the boss. "*Fuck.*"

Both men ignored her as they stood several feet away beside the dining table. She pushed herself up until she was sitting upright, and took in the cabin around her. It was a small space, with a kitchen in one corner, this sofa and an additional arm chair, and the dining table surrounded by four spindle-backed chairs. She twisted to look behind her to see a short hallway between two additional rooms – she'd guess a bedroom and bathroom. The floors, wall and ceiling were all solid wood, broken up by whimsical curtains, a couple of large floor rugs, an unlit stone fireplace and some large faded framed art prints of mountain peaks.

It would all be adorably cozy and quaint if she wasn't being held against her will.

"I'll change the meeting time," the boss grunted.

"He'll be pissed," replied the brute.

"Got any other insights, genius?"

The brute shrugged. "Use one of our cell phones instead?"

The boss pushed back his hoodie. Violet didn't know what it meant that these men were allowing her to see their faces. "You want *your* cell associated with this shit? Or an encrypted laptop some tech mastermind has set up especially?"

Tech mastermind?

Violet was *so* over having no goddamn idea what was going on. An encrypted laptop? A meeting?

What had any of this to do with her?

Something caught her gaze – the glint of the van's key sitting on the faux marble kitchen countertop. *That's* what she needed to get out of here: those keys.

But a moment later the boss snatched them up before turning back to the brute.

"Don't let her out of your sight. I'll be back."

THE TRUCK HAD RED PEELING paint and an unidentified rattling noise coming from the back seat, but Andy didn't care. It was driving him closer to Violet.

Maybe. Or maybe he was going in totally the wrong fucking direction.

He gripped the truck's steering wheel hard. He'd hired it for a fee that was frankly extortionate but he'd pay it again in an instant. It had taken mere minutes to negotiate a price and transfer the funds to the balding watch-researcher through his online bank account, but it had felt like hours.

Where was Violet?

He could still hear the echoes of her screams as he'd been dragged across that bridge and thrown into the river.

He'd floored it when he'd hit the interstate, but was very much aware he had no idea where he was going. A few months' back Sam Taberner had done something similar – jumped in his truck and driven randomly in search of a woman. At the time Andy hadn't understood – but now he got it. Sure, he *could* sit on his ass and wait for the Shadow Team to see his email and then for Shadow Ops to start weaving their intel magic. That was probably a more sensible, logical way to approach the search for Violet. After all, with every passing mile he could be driving further away from her. Further away so that when Shadow Ops finally spun into action he might be too far away. Too late to do anything.

But there was nothing sensible or logical in Andy's brain when it came to Violet. There never had been. There probably never would, despite his fucked-up efforts to do the right thing when it came to her.

Not that any of that mattered now.

He flew along the deserted interstate in the darkness.

Violet, I'll find you.

SOMEHOW, she dozed.

On the lumpy sofa while her creepy guard watched some violent movie on his phone at the dining table.

After the boss left she'd watched the brute warily, but he seemed to be taking the *no touching* rule seriously and he kept his distance. With no vehicle to escape in, and no immediate threat, exhaustion made her eyelids heavy.

She fought it at first. Surely falling asleep while being kidnapped wasn't smart? Or on the other hand - maybe resting while she was relatively safe was, in fact, a clever thing to do? She tried to analyze her choices, wishing this was a decision she could make with one of her much-loved spreadsheets.

Exhaustion decided for her anyway, and as she dozed she lamented the fact that of the many self-help audiobooks she listened to while hiking through the woods that surrounded Falcon, she'd never listened to any that explained what to do if one was kidnapped. Productivity, organization, mindfulness... her usual topics of choice were of no help whatsoever. A daily affirmation wasn't going to help her overpower the boss and the brute, was it?

That ridiculous thought made her chuckle, only for her laugh to hitch into a sob as she thought of Andy.

Feels like a dream to have you... he'd said.

The man who'd filled her dreams – day and night – *couldn't* be gone. He was so much: so big, so strong, so damn *stubborn* – how could he be dead?

She sobbed again.

The brute turned the volume up on his phone.

Her eyes slid shut. She slept.

. . .

He was going the wrong way.

The realization came from nowhere about two hours into his journey west on the I-70.

Andy pulled over so abruptly the old red truck bounced over the curb as he drove into a gas station parking lot where the interstate met Grand Junction, Colorado. It was 2am and he was alone as he filled the truck's gas tank.

The fluorescent lights of a Wienerschnitzel sign flickered as he went into the store to pay, and his stomach roiled at the scent of chili cheese dog. He stabbed at the button to make himself a black coffee at the coffee bar and rubbed his forehead as the machine whirred to life.

Wrong way.

The nature of his career – both now and in the special forces – meant that Andy was used to making decisions based on carefully researched intelligence and years of specialized training. As a Delta Force and now Shadow Team operator he often had the lives of innocents – hostages, civilians – in his hands. And also the lives of his team mates. He didn't make decisions based on a random gut feeling. He made decisions based on years of experience, well-drilled tactics and training, and the best intelligence in the world.

Except once – at the Fox & Laughton five years ago.

His coffee cup was full, and he firmly attached its lid before carrying it to the register.

The gas station was brightly lit and full with the garish colors of advertising and food packaging. It was the polar opposite of a hotel under siege with no power. It was nothing like that night where he'd herded a group of terrified tourists down one hallway in the darkness... and then changed his mind. At the time it was inexplicable.

He'd argued with Dev – a whispered, urgent conversation.

And he'd gone one way and Dev the other.

He'd made the right decision. Dev... well Andy knew Dev still lived with the heavy weight of his decision.

Right now was nothing like that night... but also everything like it.

A woman's life was at stake, and he had *no fucking idea what to do.*

In that damn hotel they'd had nothing, either. They'd had nothing to guide them but gut instinct that had both worked and been fucking disastrous in equal measures.

Wrong way.

He paid, then went back to the truck. But he didn't drive it far – he simply parked it in a bay beside the interstate, sipped his coffee and checked his email.

Nothing yet from the Shadow Team.

He considered – and dismissed – calling the cops. At least for now. He had nothing for the cops to go on for one thing – he wasn't even certain the van had been black, and his descriptions of the kidnappers would be equally useless: two men wearing hoodies. But secondly, Shadow Ops would *instantly* move into motion, whereas the local deputies would likely be as skeptical as the crew at the Lava Bar & Grill – and lack easy access to the technology needed to search for Violet.

He refreshed his email again. Still nothing.

Andy didn't head back the way he came. His gut might be telling him he'd gone too far down the interstate, but that's all he had. He'd passed dozens of exits on the I-70, and he couldn't risk taking the wrong one...

He lasted two minutes sitting still in that truck.

No. Nope. He could not sit on his ass while Violet was missing.

Five minutes after he peeled out east on the interstate, his cell rang.

VIOLET WOKE to the boss and the brute bickering over the laptop, and a full bladder.

Early morning light filtered through the drawn curtains.

"I need to use the bathroom," she said.

Both men turned to face her, their gazes dropping to her bound wrists. Surely they'd untie her to let her pee?

The brute's eyes lit up. "I'll help!"

Violet recoiled against the back of the couch.

The boss shook his head. "Fuck sake, man. We want to get our cash, we follow the rules." He reached into his back pocket to extract the same blade he'd threatened her with last night. He sauntered over but paused before reaching for her wrists.

"Lady," he said. "Don't you get any ideas. Same deal as before. You behave, you're going home. The old lady is unharmed."

She nodded. But had her gaze drifted to where the van keys had been left on the kitchen counter?

The boss sighed, then tugged up his hoodie high enough that she could see what was shoved into the front pocket of his jeans: a black handgun.

"Miss Chapman," he said, almost formally this time. "I need to be absolutely clear now. If you run away from this cabin I will shoot you between the shoulder blades as easily as I tossed your boyfriend into the Colorado river. It's not our client's preferred end to this situation, but he's not ruled it out."

Her throat closed over at the casual mention of Andy.

"Who—" she attempted; her words strangled. She cleared her throat. "Who *is* your client? What does he want with me?" Her voice shook with frustration. "What *is* this situation?"

The boss ignored her as he grabbed her hands and sliced through the zip tie.

He stepped back and gestured to the bathroom behind her. "All will be revealed in..." he glanced at his watch. "...approximately five minutes. Better hurry up."

ELEVEN

Even with all the resources of Shadow Operations behind them, everything just took too fucking long.

Andy sat in his red truck outside The Mercantile in Guneo, Colorado, a small agricultural town in the White River valley as he waited for the latest update from Shadow Ops.

He was here thanks to an extraordinary stroke of luck – Shadow Ops had tracked his lost phone, which appeared to still be onboard the van he only vaguely remembered. But either his cell battery had died, or the van had gone off the grid – which was very possible given Guneo's proximity to the Flat Tops Wilderness area – as the signal had now been lost. But his phone had proven he'd been right – he'd overshot Violet as he'd headed to Grand Junction, instead of turning north into the mountains about 45 miles out from the Lava Bar. So, assuming

Violet had been in the vicinity of his phone, she'd been *right here* not even an hour ago.

He looked up and down the nearly deserted street for the thousandth time – but there was no familiar shock of red hair. There was no black van.

There was absolutely fucking nothing.

Apart from the location of his phone, Shadow Ops also had absolutely nothing. They hadn't yet found any footage of the van in Falcon – so they didn't know even the model of the van, let alone the license plate.

In theory he was waiting for the local sheriff's department to turn up to gain permission to view the security footage from The Mercantile and the gas station, the only two businesses in this tiny community.

This was often how The Shadow Team worked – through a network of trusted, senior law enforcement, military or government officials Shadow Operations had access to an incredibly powerful network. Sometimes the simple things – for example a local cop asking a small business owner to turn over security footage – was far more efficient than Shadow Ops hacking into the supposedly secure cloud network where that footage was stored.

All very sensible, of course, until someone you cared about was in danger.

Someone I care about?

He remembered how he'd felt when he thought he'd been dreaming. When he'd thought he'd capitulated and Violet was finally in his bed.

It had felt so damn good. So damn *right*. So much more than simply *caring*.

He got out of his truck. There was still no sign of the sheriff but he didn't give a shit. It was just before 6am, and a woman with salt and pepper hair in a high ponytail was opening The Mercantile. She rolled a planter box on wheels outside as he approached; the planter full of colorful pansies.

Her expression was wary.

He got that. He still wore the clothes he'd been dunked in the river in, although he was no longer soaked through thanks to a threadbare towel he'd found in the bed of the truck, and the truck's surprisingly effective heater. But he was bedraggled and definitely smelt a bit like river water - and he couldn't suddenly make himself physically smaller or erase the bruises on his face. At 6'2" he loomed over the 50-something woman, and his attempt at a friendly smile was clearly ineffective.

She took three swift steps back towards the door.

"Please," he said, "it's important."

"No thank you," she muttered. "I've had enough of men and their *important* demands today."

"What other men?" he asked, as she swept through the shop entrance. "Were they here about an hour ago?"

She didn't look back. "You're welcome to browse the mercantile. Stock feed is out the back, and there's some lovely new seedlings in the greenhouse."

The woman skirted behind the shop counter and her shoulders instantly relaxed. He bet she had a shotgun somewhere beneath the register, the way her gaze kept dropping downwards.

"Who made you so jittery?" he asked.

She crossed her arms. "I don't want any trouble."

"I'm not trouble."

Her gaze flicked up and down his body. "Yes sir, you are."

"No, I'm not."

She raised an eyebrow. "We're playing that game?"

Andy took a deep breath. He should go back outside, leave this woman alone and wait for the Sheriff.

But how the hell could he wait when every second might count? Right now... *right this instant*... what was happening to Violet?

"The man you saw, what did he want?"

"There was no man," she replied firmly. "You misheard me."

"Understood," Andy said. "But if there was, what did he want?"

She shook her head, her complexion pale. "I should never have said *anything*," she said faintly, "he said... I mean... I *can't*." She straightened her shoulders. "I won't."

He ran a hand through his hair. It was dry now, but blood still matted the wound on the back of his skull. This woman had clearly been threatened. He wasn't getting anywhere here – he couldn't force her to tell him what she knew. He'd have to wait, as much as it killed him.

His cell phone rang, and he stepped away from the counter as he answered, standing beside a display of brightly colored children's suede half-chaps.

It was Shadow Ops. "ETA is now another thirty

minutes or so, all on-duty deputies were at a wreck near White River City. We've started work getting access to footage ourselves, but we're unlikely to be any faster."

Half an hour.

Andy turned back to the counter.

"Please," he said, and it shocked him how his voice shook. "That man who's made you jittery, I think he's the man who kidnapped my..." He swallowed. "Who kidnapped Violet."

"If anyone's been kidnapped," the woman said, fussing with some papers on the counter top, "I'd say the smart thing to do would be to call the police."

"Done that," Andy said. "But I don't have time to wait for them to get here."

"Sure," the woman huffed. "Whatever."

"*No,*" Andy said, trying to hold himself together. "It's not whatever. She's..." He took a deep breath. "Please, I need to know what happened if it will help me find her. If I wait," his voice cracked. "It could be too late."

She shook her head. "This is too much drama for me," she said. "I'm glad officers are coming. I'll gladly speak to *them*."

"You would?" Andy asked, as he had an idea.

He called Shadow Ops back. "Can you have one of the deputies call The Mercantile and vouch for me?"

He looked at the woman as he hung up. "Please just answer the call you're about to receive."

Her lips formed into a straight line.

It took less than a minute for a tinny ring to fill the

air, yet Andy felt like the velocity of his heart might break his ribs.

The woman answered it. For the first time he noticed the name tag on her check shirt: Prue.

Her eyes widened. "He's a what?" Then she nodded and hung up.

"Why didn't you say you're with the FBI," she said accusingly.

Andy shrugged. Until this second he'd had no idea what cover story had been fed to the White River City Sheriff's Department. Usually it didn't matter – his role was in the shadows. "You would've believed me?"

She frowned. "If my Marcus hadn't gone to school with Deputy Foster and I knew his voice as well as my son's, I wouldn't be believing it now," she said. "You look like you crawled out of a swamp."

"I need you to tell me everything you know, and show me your security footage," he said. "Now." Then a beat later. "Please."

"I don't know anything," she said firmly. "And there is no security footage from last night. Somehow, I accidentally deleted the last twenty-four hours."

"But you said—"

"This is exactly what I will tell the police when they arrive."

His jaw shook it was so tense.

"A woman's *life* is at stake—"

"Mine?" she asked. "Because *mine* is my primary concern. So, I'm not telling anyone anything. FBI. The deputies. Cops. Anyone."

He gripped the edge of the counter and the woman scuttled backwards. "*Please,*" he said, his anguish thickening his voice. "Violet, she's..."

Prue shook her head.

He staggered back from the counter as hopelessness overwhelmed him. He rubbed at his eyes as he tried to pull himself together.

"You're crying?" the woman asked, her voice suddenly softer than before.

He jerked his head up to meet her gaze as he wiped at his face. His cheeks were dry, but his eyes felt raw.

When was the last time he cried?

Years ago, he thought. When he'd arrived home from the Fox & Laughton siege and Natalie had wrapped her arms around him. But not since then. Not after his relationship fell apart. Definitely not when his piece of shit father had died.

"You love her?" Prue prompted, stepping closer. "This Violet?"

Automatically he shook his head. "I can't," he said. "I haven't even kissed her."

The woman chuckled.

"I *care* about her," he continued, but the word sounded as pathetic as when he'd thought it before. "We work together."

"She's in the FBI?"

He remembered to nod. "In a way. Our office manager."

"So she's *just* a work colleague?"

"*No,*" he said firmly. "She's Violet. She's..." He

searched for the right words. If he could make Prue understand who Violet was, would she help? "She's smart and feisty. She never takes a step back from anything. She is super organized and bossy, and she's forever trying to pull me into line and it's infuriating but also..." He rubbed his forehead, then swallowed. "She's fire and laughter. She's gorgeous and blunt. She's methodical but playful. She's... everything." He swallowed again. "I guess."

"You guess," Prue said, knotting her fingers together.

Andy's throat was tight as he waited.

"The gas station's cameras haven't recorded anything in years," she said eventually. "That won't help you. But..." She rubbed her palms on her thighs. "Can you send someone, like a guard? To protect me?"

"Yes," he said. "I'll organize it straight away."

She nodded. Another long, endless minute passed.

"I live in an apartment out the back," she said, finally. "Never had much trouble. Some kids shoplifting. Once an asshole ex-husband came and threatened one of my staff, but the deputies dealt with that." Andy noticed her hands had begun to shake. "An hour or so ago, like you said, someone broke into the store. I heard the noise, not realizing what it was, and came out to investigate, and this *man* was just in here. He pulled a gun on me in my pajamas. Made me help him find what he wanted, then he watched me delete the security camera footage then cut the wires to the hard drive that stores the footage so nothing new would be recorded." She took a deep breath. "Then he told me if I told anyone anything about what had just happened, he'd shoot me as I slept." She swallowed. "Maybe I didn't look like I believed him, and at that stage I *definitely* planned to tell the Sheriff. I'm as law-abiding as they come you understand?" She took another long, deep breath. Then another. "He made me watch a video on his phone that clearly showed him... um..." She gave a little hiccup. "*Executing* someone. He made me watch him shooting a man in the head. *Shooting a man in the head.*"

She grabbed a tissue from a box on the counter and blew her nose.

She looked at Andy through tears.

"I don't want to have that happen to me, sir," she said. "But I also don't want it to happen to your Violet. Was easier not to tell you when I thought you were a swamp monster, not some lovesick fool. I can't have that on my conscience."

Despite everything, he swallowed his automatic reaction: *I'm not lovesick...* Her misunderstanding was not important right now.

"Thank you," he said instead. "I promise you'll be kept safe until this is over." Dev, Tabs and Grey were already on their way to Guneo. Either one of them, or a local deputy, would stay with Prue. "What did the man want?"

She gave a weepy laugh. "A universal laptop charger, would you believe?"

"And where did he go?"

She shook her head. "I don't know exactly." She reached beneath the counter and then shoved a scrap of paper across the surface to Andy. "But this is the license number. I wrote it down more so I'd know if I ever saw the van again. I'm pretty sure it was a black Ford Transit." She met Andy's gaze. "I watched him drive away," she continued. "He headed that way down the highway," she said, gesturing east, "and I watched his tail lights for ages – because of the slopes of the mountains I could watch for some distance. I wanted to make sure he wasn't coming back." She shrugged. "It's probably not much help, but I think he turned on the gravel road just past Guneo Creek, as there's a rise just past there where I should've seen the van's tail lights again, but I didn't. There's several homes near the highway, but further up are a few cabins used by hunters and tourists, and a campground."

"*Thank you,*" he breathed, already moving towards the door. "Lock up behind me and make sure that gun you've got beneath the counter is loaded. Don't open the door for anyone other than your local deputies when they get here, got it?"

She nodded nervously, then lifted her chin. "Go get your girl."

"She's not—" he began, as he broke into a run.

Laughter followed him out the front door.

TWELVE

THE BRUTE TIED VIOLET TO ONE OF THE SPINDLE-back chairs, each wrist secured with a zip tie awkwardly behind her back, and plonked the laptop in front of her.

On the screen she could see herself. She was the only attendee in a web conference, the laptop camera streaming an image of her wild hair, and her makeup in streaks down her face from crying.

She'd been kidnapped to attend a Zoom meeting? Seriously?

Someone else entered the meeting, and as their face – their familiar face – appeared, she jerked back in shock.

"Matt?" she gasped incredulously at her New York ex-boyfriend. "Have they kidnapped you, too?"

He laughed. *Laughed.* And it was that self-satisfied, smug laugh of his that she'd always hated. He'd used it whenever she was wrong, no matter how insignificant the error – say mis-remembering the name of a coffee shop.

Or getting the departure time of their flight wrong by five minutes.

Why was he laughing? Why—

Matt had not been kidnapped. That smug expression made that abundantly clear. That lead to only one possible conclusion.

"Why the fuck did you kidnap *me*?" she asked, her voice an anguished screech. Never in a million, trillion years would she have thought Matt McKendrick capable of anything like this.

"You know why," he said calmly. She recognized this tone, too, and it made her skin crawl. Had he always been this patronizing?

"No, I don't," she said.

He rolled his eyes. "Oh Violet, no need to pretend."

Why on earth had she been so devastated when he'd dumped her? Looking at him now, she couldn't even remember why she'd been attracted to him in the first place. He was so damn neat in his white polo shirt and close-cropped blond hair, while his frame was sparce and narrow, nothing at all like Andy...

Andy.

"The men who kidnapped me, they...*hurt*... a man." She couldn't make herself verbalize, let alone think, that Andy had likely been murdered.

Matt shrugged. "I'm quite aware of that complication," he said blandly. "My men have kept me informed."

"But Andy—"

He shook his head impatiently. "I don't give a shit about the dude you're fucking, Violet. What I care about is my business." He paused before continuing briskly. "Now, let's get to the point. I cannot have you messing around with my software any longer."

"What software?"

The only software she used regularly was to create spreadsheets.

Matt sighed. "You're a smart woman, Violet. I always thought this might happen again, but I'd really hoped it wouldn't."

Again?

"I honestly have no idea what you're talking about."

Her words seemed to finally sink in as Matt studied her properly. She remembered this too, his inability to take notice of her emotions.

Suddenly, he gave a bark of laughter. As smug as before, but now even more loud and obnoxious.

"Oh, this is *too good*," he guffawed. "All this effort for nothing. Here I was thinking you were being your data wizard self, and you have no fucking idea. Just happily bumbling around in bum-fuck nowhere in Colorado, diligently managing the finances for your dear little County Fair." He clapped his hand to his lips. "This is both amazing and awful," he said, suddenly sobering. "I've clearly wasted a lot of time and money on getting you to this cabin, but hey—" he shrugged, "—while you're here and all that..."

"Wait," she interrupted, as an idea formed. She *had* used new software this week. "The software I've set up for the Rodeo Committee, it's the non-profit version of the enterprise financial software we used at Curtis Pharmaceuticals. Is *that* the software you're talking about?"

He nodded, that smug smile back.

"What do you mean *messing around in my software again?*" she asked.

His smile broadened. "Think, Violet. Give me faith I wasn't totally wrong about you. You *can't* be this stupid."

She glared at him. "I'm *not* stupid—"

Wait.

When was the last time she'd messed around with *any* data using that financial software, before this week? It'd been only a few days prior to her appalling, drunken behavior that ended her career. When compared to *that* humiliation, her smaller humiliation a few days earlier had paled in comparison.

"I extracted and analyzed data from that software the week I was fired," she said quietly. "After I noticed some minor discrepancies in my dashboards."

"Which you discussed with me," he said calmly. "At dinner at that sushi bar on West 28th Street."

"But when I escalated it at Curtis Pharmaceuticals, the data in the report I put forward was wrong when cross checked. It looked like I'd made an embarrassingly basic error in my calculations, and caused significant stress to the Exec Team because of what I *thought* I'd discovered – that money was being skimmed from the company's accounts. Hundreds of thousands of dollars."

Another smug nod from Matt.

"But I was right, wasn't I?" she said, her words

gaining momentum as her understanding grew. "My data *was* correct." Despite her situation, her lips quirked at that realization. She'd been *right*. "But – you don't work for that finance software company? You worked remotely for some startup in Silicon Valley. What did you have to do with any of it?"

He settled back in his chair. She recognized the drawn striped drapes behind his seat – he still lived in the apartment they'd once shared in Midtown.

"I'm my own startup," he said. "Always have been. I contracted a bit for that Silicon Valley tech company but really it was just a front. I always had an idea, and when I met you, I found a way to test it out." He laughed. "Honestly, who is dumb enough to use the same password for everything? Was easy as pie to get into the Curtis network. Took me a bit longer to expose all the security vulnerabilities in the financial software, but with everything in the cloud now it wasn't all that difficult."

"You dated me for my passwords?"

"And because I thought you were hot in your nerdy little way." He wrinkled his nose. "Don't like the idea of you with that neanderthal dude though. You've dropped your standards."

If her hands were free she would've grabbed the laptop and thrown it against a wall. "Don't you *dare* speak about Andy like that. He is ten times... a million times the man you are."

He shrugged. "At least I'm alive."

At that, she screamed at him. "You absolute shit stain of a man—"

A blow to the side of her head abruptly silenced her. Without her hands to steady her, her chair wobbled precariously before settling upright again. Her ears ringing, it took long moments for her vision to re-focus on Matt on the screen. Beside her the brute stood close, clearly ready to strike her again.

"No yelling," Matt said. "Can't risk the off chance that a ladies book club on their little off-the-grid wilderness retreat hears a ruckus."

She took several deep breaths as the pain gradually subsided.

"It's called salami-slicing," Matt continued coolly, as if he hadn't just directed a man to assault her. "It's been around since at least the 1990s, but it's a classic move. Simply write code that diverts tiny amounts of money from a business account to, well, mine." He laughed. "It's harder nowadays to create something utterly undetectable – but I've done it."

"I detected it," she said.

His eyes narrowed. "No," he said firmly. "You noticed a rookie error in an early version of the software. That's now been addressed."

"Yet you kidnapped me because you thought I was going to find evidence of what you were doing...again."

Matt nodded in the brute's direction, and she had no chance to brace before another blow smacked against the side of her head. This time the force of the slap toppled her chair to the ground, and without her hands to slow her fall, her shoulder took the brunt of her weight.

She cried out in pain.

Quickly her seat was jerked upright again, her fallen glasses roughly shoved back on.

Matt smirked back at her through the screen. "Don't be a smart ass, Vi," he said gently. "Curtis Pharmaceuticals was my sandpit. Now I've expanded. My software is installed in dozens of massive corporations and I'm making millions."

Finally, she looked at the man in front of her *not* as her ex-boyfriend, but as what he was: a monster. A monster who had no qualms to hurt her, or hurt others. Matt was far more dangerous than the kidnappers in the cabin. He would do anything to protect his money.

Anything.

Suddenly a goddamn avalanche of puzzle pieces clicked together. Pieces that she hadn't fully comprehended were missing from the puzzle of her inexcusable behavior back in New York.

She gasped.

"Oh, there it is!" Matt crowed. "You finally worked it out. Brilliant, wasn't it?"

"You staged everything," she said carefully as horror dawned. "That wild night that ended up in the boardroom... I didn't do any of that?"

"Of course not. I paid a bartender to put rohypnol in your drinks. He fucked up with that Head of IT though, I'd picked out a single guy from Curtis originally, but the stupid bartender couldn't tell them apart. I for sure thought you'd know you'd never fuck that IT loser, but I guess your founding years in Falcon thinking you were total white trash really did a number on you, hey? It was so easy for you to believe you'd fuck a married guy at your place of work." He shook his head. "Made listening to all your boring-as-shit whining about your mom and that stupid town worthwhile though! Worked a treat."

Bile pooled in her throat. Matt had used her greatest insecurities to destroy her.

"You ruined my professional reputation. My *life*."

He shrugged. "I'm talking *millions* on the line here, Vi. Billions, even, one day." He smiled. "But look, let's cut to the chase. Seems I was a bit premature thinking you were onto me. But the fact is, it was always a risk, especially once I knew you were using that financial software again." He paused to answer the question he must've seen on her face. "I monitor user logs, specifically for your name and email address, but also your location. There isn't a lot of activity coming out of Falcon for me to follow up."

So, despite ruining her life, Matt had continued to see her as a threat.

"I brought you here today, Violet, to be crystal clear about what I need you to do from now on, and that's simple. *Do not fuck this up for me.* Never go data mining where you aren't wanted, and that means *never* attempting to return to your career. I have big plans for my salami-slicing, and I can't be keeping you up to date with all the software I've hacked, so it's easier if you just stay the hell away from data. Got it?"

It was clearly a rhetorical question.

"Next, *never* mention any of this to anyone. Never discuss what I've told you today, never discuss what happened at Curtis Pharmaceuticals. Ever. That means the cops, your deadbeat mom, your sweet-as-pie Nanna, or the next lump of testosterone you choose to fuck at that dinky auto-repair shop." He looked at the brute standing beside her. "Put your hand on her shoulder," he directed.

The brute's meaty hand gripped her shoulder hard, and she flinched. A combination of the pain of the man's hand on the still forming bruises from her fall, and simply the reality of his unwanted touch.

"See, Violet? I'll be right *there*, all the time," he said. "And if you do the wrong thing, I'll order the death of your dear Nanna. There'll be no warning. I'll find out, and it will happen. And after your Nanna it will be... maybe your pretty friend, Casey?"

She didn't react at all. What was the point?

Minutes ago she'd been perversely buoyed by the discovery of what Matt had done to her. It meant so much to know she'd been right about those data errors, and that her boardroom scandal was all fake. She'd been carrying guilt and shame for more than a year... and just like that, it was gone. And replaced by a white-hot fury.

But what could she do with her re-found confidence in herself? With her anger?

Nothing. Or the people she most loved would die.

The brute squeezed her shoulder, dragging her attention back to Matt.

"And if you ever have kids with one of those auto-shop dumbasses, then they'll go straight to the top of my list. Got it? You'll always be last. After *everyone* you love and care about." He shrugged. "And you know I'll do it. Given what happened to your dear Andy today."

"Why not just kill me now?" she asked, desolate. "Or before, back in New York?"

Another smug, awful laugh. "Oh no," he said. "I couldn't do that. I'll always have a soft spot for you." He sneered. "I always liked looking down at your glorious hair when you sucked my cock." He spoke like they were having a perfectly sensible conversation. "And I still use some of the fancy spreadsheets you made me. No," he continued, "my strong preference is to have you alive and well, just staying the fuck away from me and my money." His gaze, once again, drifted to the brute. A few feet to the brute's left stood the boss. "As I said," he said, speaking to the kidnappers. "Do *not* touch. Got it?"

Both men nodded.

"So!" Matt said, "I think we're all clear where we stand. Correct, Violet?"

Somehow Violet managed to nod.

"Fantastic!" Matt said, before waving and abruptly disconnecting from the meeting.

Violet was vaguely aware of the boss switching off the laptop, and both men having a murmured conversation.

She just sat there, stunned. Trying to make sense of what she'd just discovered. Trying to make sense of the past twelve months.

And then she felt the zip tie give way on one of her wrists. She looked up to see the boss only inches away from her. He rubbed the delicate veins of her wrist with his thumb, but held firm when she tried to snatch her hand away.

"Matt might've claimed what happened to your boyfriend," The Boss said in a low, menacing tone, "but you know who was responsible. So, I'm telling you now. You're coming with us to the bedroom, and you're going to be *real nice* to us. Got it? And you're not going to be telling Mr Salami Slicer. Because if you do, I promise your Nanna won't live through the night."

"No!" she said, scrambling to her feet.

No. This couldn't be happening.

One wrist was still tied tight to the chair, and it dragged noisily on the floorboards as she backed away from the men.

The boss rolled his eyes. "We can do this at gunpoint, lady."

She bent down to grab the chair leg with her free hand so she was holding it like a shield in front of her. "*No*," she said again.

The men glanced at each other and nodded.

Then together, they came at her.

She screamed.

THIRTEEN

Near the highway the homes on that first left after Guneo Creek were reasonably close together, each on maybe an acre or two of land. All were privately owned, with one place complete with children laughing raucously as they raced up and down the driveway on their BMXs in the early morning sun.

In the few minutes it had taken Andy to drive from the mercantile to this gravel road, Shadow Ops had completed a global database search of each property, mining for any information they had access to. A Shadow Ops analyst provided him with information as he drove past each place through his cell phone speaker.

"22104 has had same owner for the last ten years. One speeding ticket nineteen years ago, otherwise no criminal record," she said, her tone efficient. "22105 is currently rented. Long term tenant, he manages the Family Dollar next town over."

And so it continued as he wound his way higher into

the mountains, the gravel pinging in a steady pattern against the fading red paint of his borrowed truck. The analyst perused satellite photographs as she spoke, but the latest images were several days old – unfortunately real-time satellite images of this part of rural Colorado just didn't exist. But there were still far more recent than anything available on your standard maps app. She was searching for any unexpected structures or anything else unusual. But close to the highway, everything seemed utterly normal.

Of course, Violet *could* be trapped within any of those utterly normal homes, but he didn't have the time – or the authority – to search each and every house. It killed him to simply drive by based on the advice of the Shadow Ops analysts, but there was no other option. Now he had a van description and license plate, Shadow Ops had swung into action, and roadblocks were being put in place thanks to local law enforcement. The remainder of the Shadow Team were already half way to Guneo – but none of this was of any use to Andy – or Violet – right this second. He needed to get to Violet *now*, not when re-enforcements arrived.

The first property he searched was maybe twenty minutes from the highway. Up here, the lots were dotted with spruce trees and firs in contrast to the rolling cleared fields that surrounded the town below. The house was only fifty feet from the gravel road, and supposedly vacant – an Air BnB that currently had no visitors.

He approached on foot, unarmed, as he'd no opportunity to acquire a firearm beyond a brief attempt to purchase the barman's handgun at the Lava Bar. Unsurprisingly the man had been unwilling to hand over a loaded weapon to a soaking wet and bleeding stranger in the middle of the night.

The property – a renovated antique train carriage – was empty. Andy sprinted back to his truck and began his journey again. Ten minutes further up the road and his cell phone coverage began to crackle. But by now he'd been sent details of all properties along the gravel road, with a cluster of three near the end determined the most likely locations to find Violet. All three were off the grid and totally private, each cabin several hundred feet from the road. Up here, as the voice of the Shadow Ops Analyst finally cut out completely, the terrain was steep and densely wooded. The cabins he was heading for were advertised to both hunters and tourists – one was occupied, the other two vacant.

Would the assholes who'd kidnapped Violet just simply book a cabin to hold her hostage? Who knew. But as Andy drove deeper into the woods, he felt certain he was heading in the right direction.

Violet is up here.

He parked at the side of the road of the first property – the occupied cabin. This was a larger, sprawling building, painted white – and he hadn't walked far before he could see it through the trees.

Parked in front of the white wooden cabin were four different cars – all SUVs with kid-related bumper stickers. As he hid behind the cover of a nest of silver poplars, a woman laughed somewhere in the distance, quickly joined by another.

Andy swiftly made his retreat. Violet wasn't here.

She wasn't at the next cabin either, and he wasted long minutes stalking his way along a narrow half-mile dirt driveway to approach the rustic log cabin with caution. The place was totally barren, excluding a small herd of deer he'd disturbed grazing beyond the (empty) garage.

With every passing moment he grew more tense, and it became increasingly difficult to quieten the roar of panic in his ears. He slapped his hand against the empty cabin's garage door in frustration, the sudden noise startling a family of doves roosting in the gutters. Then he turned and ran back to the road.

The next cabin was near enough he could remain on foot, and his boots skidded on the gravel road as he sprinted up the steep incline towards its entrance, not allowing himself to consider the possibility Violet wasn't at his next destination either. Or that he was already too late.

His heart was beating hard – and it had nothing to do with exertion.

I'm coming Violet, I'm coming.

Then, he heard the screaming.

Violet screamed as she ran at the boss, smacking him in the gut with the full force of the wooden chair. He fell to the ground, cursing, as she turned to face the brute.

He smirked. "You really think this is going to work?" he drawled.

She ran at him, too, but the brute was ready, and he grabbed two chair legs, effectively trapping her. She pulled back on her zip tie, clawing at it with her free hand, desperately trying to twist her hand free.

She didn't stop screaming. She swore at them both, giving voice to her fear and her fury.

"You fucking pieces of shit! I'm not playing nice. I'm not making anything fucking easy for you..."

She gasped as the boss grabbed her from behind, wrapping his arms around her body and trapping her spare arm hard against her side. She kicked and squirmed, never stopping her stream of screamed obscenities. She suspected Matt's mention of a nearby book club was facetious, but maybe there *was* someone nearby. Maybe someone would hear.

She refused to not at least try.

She didn't stop fighting as the brute grabbed a blade from his pocket to cut through her zip ties.

"Stay still you silly bitch," he muttered.

She did not stay still.

For a moment her hand was free and she swung it wildly over her shoulder, her fist glancing off the jaw of the man behind her. He simply yanked her harder against him.

"*Bad girl*," he seethed against her ear, before effortlessly grabbing her free arm and trapping both arms behind her back.

When the brute made a grab for her breasts she

kicked out, catching his shin with her bare toes. It definitely hurt her more than him, and he laughed. He looked over her shoulder at the boss behind her. "Probably easiest if we tie her to the bed?" he asked, calmly stepping out of reach of her flailing legs.

The boss grunted behind her as her heels battered against his legs, and as she uselessly stomped against his boots, screaming all the time.

No. No, no, no, no, no.

She fought as she was dragged across the room. She could feel the hardness of the boss's handgun at her back. If she could get free, could she somehow twist and grab it?

Panicked thoughts tumbled through her head as she desperately tried to work out a plan, work out *anything* that would save her. They were in the small hallway, the brute a step ahead, shoving the door open to make way for her.

She kept on fighting, kept on yelling.

They'll have to let me go at some point, she realized.

Seconds maybe, but if they were going to tie her, The Boss would have to loosen his grip.

As she was manhandled through the door, in her thrashing the side of her head bumped against the doorframe with a dull thunk. It stung, and she shut her eyes momentarily at the sharp pain, then had an idea.

She went still and heavy in The Boss's arms, as if she were unconscious.

"Oh, for fuck sake," The Boss groaned.

Violet let her limbs sag so she flopped forward over

the man's arms.

"At least she's shut up," the brute commented as she was dragged across the room. Her bare feet bumped over the wooden floor and a thick rug, before she was awkwardly tossed onto the bed, her upper body flung towards the pillows, her knees still hanging over the edge.

As she allowed her arms to fly upwards with her movement, she made sure that between her forearm and her hair, her face was covered. She needed to be able to see what was going on.

Her heart hammered against her ribs as she peered carefully through her hair. She could see the boss's black jean-clad legs beside the nightstand, and the brute was – she was pretty sure – standing at the end of the white metal bedframe.

She needed to get that gun. There was no way she'd ever overpower these men, or even beat them in a foot race. The gun was *key*.

"Just tie her wrists to the bed," the brute said. "Even if she wakes up, it makes it more interesting if she fights it."

Bile heaved at the man's disgusting words.

Through her hair she watched the boss reach into his pocket. It lifted his hoodie slightly, so she could see the gun's handle in his right pocket. She focused all her attention at that gun. *That's* where she needed to lunge. She'd have one chance.

Maybe it was only a 1/1000th chance, but she had to take it.

The boss swore. "Where'd I put the fucking zip ties?"

he asked.

"Kitchen counter," the brute said. "I'll get 'em."

His boots clunked away.

This was her chance. Only one man in the room. This was it.

The boss sighed, still remaining close to her. One hand rubbed the fly of his jeans as he stared at her, and again she had to control the urge to retch. The movements at his crotch became more deliberate as he reached forward, bringing himself – and the gun - closer to her as his fingers brushed against her breast.

She kept her breathing slow and steady, somehow not flinching at the man's touch. All her attention was at his right hip.

"I would've fucked you against the side of your Prius," the man grunted. "I saw what you were offering that stupid son of a bitch, and I—"

She hurled herself toward him, slamming her feet onto the floor as she reached both hands for the gun, her fingers wrapping around the handle as her momentum carried her forward.

The boss shouted and staggered backwards as she tugged with all her might, yanking the gun free.

But her grip was unsteady, and the force of her movement flung the gun away from her to clatter loud upon the floor. She pushed both hands against the boss's chest, and he was so unbalanced he fell hard against the wall. She scrambled, stumbling over the edge of the rug. She righted herself, but then the boss's hands grabbed her ankle, and she plummeted to the floor.

The gun was so close, maybe two feet from her grasp. She kicked as she tried to get to her hands and knees, and as the boss shouted out for the brute to come help.

She needed the gun before the brute came back.

She *had* to keep on moving. Her hands gripped desperately against the lush pile of the rug as she tried to shake free.

Almost. Almost.

She reached out, the gun so close. *So close.*

Then with a thud, the boss landed on her back, his hands grabbing her wrists.

"No!" but her scream was weak as his weight had knocked the air out of her lungs. She bucked and twisted beneath him, refusing to give up.

But it was useless. He was too big. Too heavy. Too strong.

"Get in here you asshole!" the boss shouted. "She's being a little bitch."

The sound of fast approaching booted feet echoed in the small cabin.

This was it. It was over. Her one chance had evaporated, just like that.

She sobbed as she continued to twist and fight. Boots came into her line of sight across the floor.

"I'd say you're the little bitch in this scenario," said the man wearing the boots.

But it wasn't the brute speaking.

She jerked her head up.

It was Andy.

FOURTEEN

ANDY HAD NEVER RUN SO FAST IN HIS LIFE.

The tiny cabin was nestled behind towering spruce trees, the black Ford Transit van parked right in front, a Satellite propped onto its roof.

Violet's screams didn't abate as he ran, and his gut twisted in torment. As he got closer, he could hear what she was saying: *You gutless pieces of shit. You're worse than shit! You're the regurgitated moose shit... that the labradoodle next door... vomits all over my Nanna's front yard...*

She was fighting. She was alive and she was fighting.

He skidded to a stop at the van, yanking a door open as he used precious seconds to search for a firearm or other weapon. Nothing.

He left the door open as he raced up the cabin's steps. He could hear the voices of both men inside, but the curtains were drawn on both of the cabin's front windows. He couldn't see inside, but likewise they had no idea he was here.

He fought the instinct to twist open the front door – but he stopped himself as he gripped the handle.

No. *Think.*

Rushing in half-cocked was directly opposed to everything he'd ever done is his career. And it wouldn't work. The men would be armed, so his greatest advantage was surprise.

He leaned close against the door, both to listen and to judge the best way to get through it. The door was solid wood, but the lock looked like the cheapest thing the owner could find at Home Depot.

He could hear boots moving on the floor, but he couldn't hear the men's words over Violet's screams. *That a girl,* he thought. *Fucking burst their eardrums.*

They were moving to the rear of the cabin. He leapt from the small porch, searching for a window on the side of the cabin he could see through. He stood on a fallen log to peer through the tiniest gap in the drawn curtains – to see the men and Violet disappear down a hallway. An instant later he was at the front door – and miraculously it was unlocked.

He twisted it opened silently and stepped inside. The main living area was empty, but then, abruptly, Violet's screaming stopped.

Dread dropped his stomach to the soles of his feet.

Violet.

Keeping to the edges of the room, he raced toward the hallway, trying to keep his weight on his toes and move as silently as possible. With his back against the far wall, he slid towards the hallway until he reached the corner. There he gradually increased his angle from the wall, slowly increasing his field of vision until he was certain the hallway was empty.

But as he went to step into the hall, a large man in a black hoodie walked into it. Andy jumped back, but he clearly hadn't been seen. Moments later, as the man stepped directly in front of him, he shoved a hand against the man's face to silence his shout before punching him hard in the solar plexus. Then, as he gasped doubled over, delivered a short, sharp blow with the side of his hand to the man's carotid artery, knocking him out instantly.

Andy caught him before he hit the floor, then dragged him aside to the sounds of a struggle in the bedroom. He leapt over the body and ran for the room.

"Get in here you asshole! She's being a little bitch."

Andy took in the scene before him. Violet, flat on her stomach on a colorful rug, a man dressed in black holding her down as she reached desperately for a Glock that lay inches from her grasp.

"I'd say you're the little bitch in this scenario," he said with bite, snatching up the firearm as Violet's beautiful green gaze met his.

"Andy?" she gasped. "You're alive!"

Tears had smudged mascara down her face, and bruises purpled her cheekbones and temples.

"Get off her," Andy said with vicious calm. "Keep your hands up."

The man let go of Violet's wrists as he eased his weight from her body. Andy kept the gun trained on the center of the man's face, fully expecting him to try something.

Which he did. Before he'd put any meaningful space between his body and Violet's, he jerked Violet up by her hair, his other hand reaching for his back pocket. A moment later a blade was at Violet's throat as he dragged her to her feet.

"Back the fuck up, lover boy," the man snapped.

Andy couldn't easily shoot with Violet so close, so he took deep breaths as he conceded a single step as he weighed up his options.

"This isn't a good idea, man," Andy said with deliberate calm. "I need you to drop that knife."

"You want your girlfriend alive?" the man said.

Violet's gaze was unbelievably strong and brave despite the knife only inches from her skin.

"*You* want to stay alive?" Andy countered.

Violet's gaze flicked downwards to the knife. As the man focused on Andy, he'd allowed the blade to move further away from Violet. It was still too damn close, of course.

The man laughed. "You even know what to do with that Glock, lover boy? Gym muscles mean fucking nothing— *oomph!*"

Violet ducked as she angled her elbow into the man's gut and tugged hard against the man's grip on her hair. She hit him once, twice, as the man recovered from his shock and that blade arced towards Violet's neck.

Crack.

He only needed one shot.

Violet leapt into his arms.

"Is he dead? Is he dead?" she said between hiccupping sobs.

Andy had shot him directly between the eyes. There was no doubt. "Yes."

She buried her face in his neck as she cried. "Oh god, oh god... I thought you were dead, Andy. I thought..."

He caught her beneath her knees so he was cradling her as he strode out of that room.

"Are you okay?" he asked urgently. "Did they hurt you, Vi?"

"They hit me a few times, but that's it," she said. "Oh Andy, *how* are you here? How are you okay?"

As she spoke her breath was warm against his skin. She was in his arms and she was alive. His throat was tight from the enormity of his relief.

In the main cabin the other kidnapper was regaining consciousness, so he reluctantly placed Violet on the sofa. For a moment she clung to him.

"I need to tie up that other asshole," he said gruffly.

She loosened her grip on his shoulders and sunk onto the couch. She nodded.

"There are zip ties over there," she said, pointing at the kitchen counter. "That's why he left the room, to get them." Her voice wobbled at the end.

He couldn't stomach thinking about what those men had planned to do to Violet.

The man secured, he patted him down, removing a

blade and a handgun. The man was groggy but even so, his gaze was defeated. *Good.*

Because it wouldn't take much of an excuse for Andy to kill this man for what he'd done to Violet – and Andy was not a man who took death lightly, or who'd ever been fully comfortable with the necessity of death in war.

"Of course he was armed, too," Violet said, watching him over the back of the sofa. "I thought I was going to get the gun and escape, but I had no chance, did I?"

"When you went quiet, I thought you were unconscious or worse," he said, leaving the bound man on the floor and striding over to Violet. "How on earth did you unarm a man who easily has 50lbs on you?"

Without really thinking about it, he swung Violet back up into his arms again. She gasped, but didn't protest. He held her close against his chest, barely able to believe she was warm and perfect in his arms.

"I pretended to be unconscious, then threw myself at him when I had the chance." She snuggled her head beneath his chin.

"Genius," he said. "You are amazing."

She gave a disbelieving laugh. "If you hadn't arrived, it wouldn't have worked."

He grabbed the van keys and both kidnapper's cell phones on the way out. It was awkward as hell to shove them into his pockets with Violet in his arms, but no way was he putting her down. But he also wasn't leaving an easy way for the remaining kidnapper to escape, because as he'd recently proven, escaping from zip ties was far from impossible. Still, the ties only needed to hold until the Shadow Team or local law enforcement arrived, which wouldn't be long.

"I don't know about that," Andy said, jogging down the porch steps. "What you did at the end there was insane. You literally ripped some of your hair out to give me space to shoot the asshole. There were strands in the dead guy's fingers. How did you know to do that?"

"I have plenty of hair," she said. "And it seemed logical to get out of the way."

"That's my analytical Violet." She was so matter of fact. "So...kind of like your recommendation to change coffee cup suppliers," he said. "Such clear logic: No drop in quality, but a clear cost saving."

Her mouth dropped open as she looked up at him. "You *did* try my coffee cups." She laughed. "My God, you're so infuriating." But he'd achieved his goal – she was smiling.

Beneath the shade of a giant spruce, he paused to properly look at her in his arms.

He wanted to erase every bruise on her skin, and he would do anything to take the fear from her gaze.

"I was so scared," she said quietly.

"Me too."

Her eyes widened. "When they kidnapped you?"

He shook his head. "No, that asshole never should've been close enough to take me down," he said. "I wasn't scared then, just pissed at myself for not noticing some weak fuck coming at me with a rock. And sure, waking up in the Colorado River wasn't great – but that's not what I meant." He swallowed. "Violet, when I realized you were tied up in that van and trapped with those pieces of shit, I've never been so scared in my life."

Her arms tightened around his neck, and he watched a tear slide down her cheek.

"Oh Violet—" he began.

"I thought you were dead," she said. "I thought you were dead, Andy, and god it hurt so bad, even though I tried to convince myself you might have survived. I didn't believe it. I thought even you weren't strong enough, or powerful enough to survive being drowned while barely conscious."

"You think I'm strong and powerful?" he teased.

She laughed as she cried. "Oh God, Andy, I *like* you."

I like you.

It was an echo of their conversation in the parking lot near The Roost not even twelve hours earlier. *I didn't mean it that I've never liked you*, Violet had said, and what had followed had been the most revelatory, and hottest, five minutes of his life.

All fucking mine, he'd told her, before coming to his senses.

But right now, on this glorious Colorado morning, nothing seemed sensible about his decision in that carpark. Maybe it was the clear mountain air. Maybe it was the utter joy he felt holding this remarkable, brave woman in his arms. But for whatever reason, while all the knotted complications were right there in his head, he was incapable of grasping their importance. At least right now.

At least while he basked in the miracle that was finding Violet alive.

Mine.

She gasped. He hadn't realized he'd spoken the word aloud.

"Mine," he murmured again.

And then he kissed her.

FIFTEEN

Mine.

His lips silenced Violet's unthinking, instinctive reply: *I'm yours.*

Andy didn't kiss her gently. He kissed her in a way that made remaining cradled in his arms impossible, and before she knew it she was pressed against the trunk of a spruce tree, his clever lips firm against hers.

She twisted her hands behind his neck, her fingers threading through his hair. He flinched slightly as she brushed against where his hair was matted – where the boss must've hit him with that rock. Horror and fury at what had transpired momentarily wrenched her lips from his.

"Are you okay?" she breathed.

"To kiss you?" he said huskily. "Vi, there is literally nothing else I'd rather be doing." He pressed a kiss near her ear. "Well, maybe I can think of a thing or two..." She laughed as he nipped and licked his way along her jaw.

"Are *you* okay," he continued, before he made his way towards her lips. "For me to kiss you?"

"There is literally nothing else I want more," she said. Then paused. "Except sex," she added, grinning. "With you, just to be clear."

He was laughing as his lips covered hers again, and Violet lost herself in sensation. As they discovered each other's lips and tongues, the nightmare of the night faded away. Everything narrowed down to Andy and how he made her feel. And not just right now, but all the time.

All that passion and emotion.

That combustible connection that had been right there from the moment they'd met.

It had all led to this moment, made even more intense by the absolute understanding that it might never have happened. That Andy could so easily have been taken from her before *this*. Before she knew how addictive he tasted, or how perfectly her height and curves aligned with his power and strength.

She kissed him like she'd never kissed another man – with all of herself. She kissed him desperately, clinging to him like she never wanted to let go... because she didn't.

"Violet..." he murmured as they broke apart for air.

She ran her hands down his shoulders, learning the shape of his arms and back, and maybe also reassuring herself he was here and okay. That he was whole and unbroken. That he was hers.

She stood on her tip toes to kiss him again, but before his lips brushed against hers, he suddenly took a step back.

Sirens were approaching.

How?

She shook her head, her brain foggy with desire but also all that had happened to her.

She frowned up at Andy. "How are they here?" she asked, confused. Then had another thought - "How did *you* know where to find me?"

"Tracked my phone," he said easily, looking down the driveway and not at her. "It must've fallen out in the van. I called the police, too, but I was already on my way."

She nodded. That made sense. "But how did you get here?"

He chuckled. "Rented a truck from a guy."

She gave a sniff, acknowledging the faint scent of... *river*. "Soaking wet in the middle of the night?"

He shrugged. "Like I said, I've never been so scared in my life."

But this time he said the words almost dismissively and without the raw honesty of before.

The flashing lights of a police cruiser came into view down the winding driveway, bouncing about with the undulations of the gravel surface.

She took a step back from Andy, starting to comprehend how the man before her had come to be here. His desperation, his urgency – his *bravery* – to get here as fast as he could and to take on her kidnappers alone and without a weapon.

It was... overwhelming what he had done for her.

Mine, he'd said.

Yet as several cruisers came to a stop and Andy

waved to indicate they were okay; something shifted in his expression.

"Andy?" she asked.

But he jogged over to an approaching officer, calling out with his hands up as he approached. She watched as he had a brief discussion with a tall, rangy police officer, and then as several cops ran to the cabin – a few to the rear - a female cop approached her with a kind and sympathetic expression.

"Let's get you checked out," the woman said quietly. "You've been through quite the ordeal."

Violet nodded as she was led toward a patrol car.

She looked over her shoulder for Andy, spotting him in intense conversation with an officer, his back to her. She just wanted a reassuring look, or a smile. Anything.

But he didn't turn around, even as the patrol car drove away.

Andy told the officers he'd drive to the Sheriff's Office to make his statement, then walked briskly down the driveway, leaving the deputies to secure the crime scene. About half way down the drive – and out of site of the cabin – a familiar voice called out from the woods.

"Looked like you and Vi were enjoying some rescue celebrations."

Caleb Grey stepped out of the foliage along with Dev and Sam. All wore muted clothing, camo tactical vests complete with firearms and ammo, as well as ear pieces to communicate with each other.

"Shut up, Grey," Andy said lightly.

Grey grinned. "Seems you had everything under control." He paused. "I meant the rescue. Although happy to provide feedback on your kissing technique. Did notice a few areas for improvement."

"Shut up, Grey." This time it was Dev who spoke. "Violet doing okay?"

"As good as can be expected," Andy began, then his lips quirked. "Although when you're talking about Violet, her version of expected is pretty incredible. I helped, but she was doing a stellar job at being a badass."

"I have no doubt," said Sam. But his expression was serious. "Be careful with her, okay?"

Andy frowned. "What does that mean?"

"Does she know about the Shadow Team?"

"No," Andy replied. "And I don't think that's what you meant."

"'Course it was," Sam said briskly. "Right. If we're not needed here, let's get back to Falcon. I left my new fiancée alone in my bed for this."

Fiancée? Did Sam mean Cherry? He'd seen the woman who'd broken Sam's heart only briefly at The Roost last night, he'd been too focused on Violet to notice much else.

The three men faded back into the woods leaving Andy alone. His boots crunched on gravel as he made his way to the rusty red truck.

Be careful with her.

Hadn't that been the point with Violet, right from the beginning?

Be careful. Keep his distance. No complications.

Violet was not for him.

He hadn't shifted in his thinking for a moment last night.

....some lovesick fool... Prue from The Mercantile had called him, and he'd instantly rejected the idea. Honestly, how damn ridiculous. He cared for Violet. And he *did* think she was all the things he'd told Prue: Smart and feisty. Fire and laughter. Because she was, objectively, all those things. That wasn't love.

But that wasn't all Prue had said.

Go get your girl

Those words, they had stuck.

Mine. All fucking mine.

In the moment before he'd kissed her outside the cabin – and before, beside her Prius - he'd believed that. Violet was *his. Mine.* All. Fucking. Mine.

Who was he kidding? He still believed that now.

He believed it in a way that had him racing across Colorado like the lovesick fool Prue had called him. That had him incapable of making calm and measured decisions at almost any point in his desperate race to find her. He regretted none of it, of course. If he'd been five minutes later...

But now, without the pounding of his heart drowning out his rational mind, his primal possessiveness sickened him. How could it not? He'd heard this bullshit before:

You belong to me, you bitch.

He could still hear his father's low, furious voice in his head.

He'd been six years old, strapped in his car seat in the backseat of a borrowed car as his father dragged his mother away from him, and back into their house in Philadelphia.

Who the hell do you think you are to try to leave me? Without me you're nothing. Don't you get that? You're my woman. That's it. That's who you are. It's all you are.

Andy wrenched open the door to the truck and slid into the driver's seat before gripping his knees as a familiar revulsion overcame him.

I'm not like him, he told himself. Just like he had after he'd left a hole in the drywall of the apartment he'd shared with Natalie, and stormed out to the sound of her sobs and pleas.

I'm not like him.

It was why he'd legally changed his surname to his mom's the moment he could.

I'm not like him.

But did he believe that?

Deep down in his soul?

No.

Not even close.

SIXTEEN

"Can you check if my Nanna is okay? And let her know I'm fine?"

It was the first thing Violet said as the patrol car drove away from the cabin.

She didn't feel overly *fine*, but still, she was infinitely more fine than she'd been thirty minutes ago, when her would-be rapist's brain had been splattered across the cabin's plank walls behind her. She'd tried not to look, but she had.

She wished she hadn't. She wished none of this had happened.

"I'll have a call put through to the Falcon County Sheriff's Office," the female deputy replied from the passenger seat. "But my understanding is that your grandmother was notified of your disappearance by local law enforcement. We've been working closely with Falcon County. A lot of people have been searching for you."

Violet hugged herself as she looked out the window. She was glad her Nanna hadn't discovered her disappearance herself, but she wasn't sure being woken by officers in the early hours of the morning was much better. Although – was there any good way to be told that strangers had broken into your home and kidnapped someone you love?

She bit her lip, wishing she was home.

"Anyone else you'd like contacted? For support, or to drive you home after you've finished speaking to detectives?" This was the deputy driving the patrol car, an older guy with salt and pepper hair.

"No," she said instantly. Who would she call? Her mom? *Ha.* Although it wouldn't be the first time she'd been at a Sheriff's Office with her mother. Just previous experience had involved her mom being the criminal, rather than the victim: disorderly conduct, possession of drug paraphernalia, that type of thing. Just what you want to be doing at age sixteen, picking your mom up from the Falcon County Jail.

It wasn't a long drive from the cabin to the County's Sheriff's Office for her witness statement. For most of it she rested her head against the car's window and let her eyelids slide shut. She was exhausted and, she guessed, in some form of shock? She didn't feel like herself, she felt both bone-tired but also restless. She felt desperate to be home in her bed and sleep – yet also felt like she wanted to run away from all of this – all that had happened last night, but also what had happened in New York last year, and even all that had happened to her as a teenager in Falcon.

And what about Andy? What about that kiss?

Her eyes popped open as the patrol car slowed as they entered a town she didn't recognize.

Kissing Andy had been the one good thing that'd come of the nightmare of her kidnapping. *God,* it'd felt so good. But the moment the patrol cars had arrived he'd withdrawn. One moment he'd called her *mine,* the next he was shoving distance between them. It infuriated Violet that she wasn't angrier at what was now clearly a pattern of... what? A change of heart?

No, that wasn't strong enough a descriptor.

Rejection. It was a pattern of rejection.

She, of all people, should be familiar with that sensation.

And it hurt. A lot of stuff hurt from last night – and not just the physical stuff: the bruises to her stomach, shoulder and the side of her head. Her body might ache, but what Matt had told her...

It was going to take her a long time to process what Matt had done to her.

She'd loved him, in a way. Of course she had – she'd *lived* with him. She'd had sex with him... and enjoyed it. Even if sex with Matt completely paled in comparison to a single kiss from Andy.

So, this man who she'd once loved and trusted, had gone to extraordinary lengths to destroy her. He'd had no qualms in making her believe she was going crazy. *He* had been the one who'd suggested she go see a doctor for her near crippling anxiety at work once she'd realized the mammoth error she'd made with that data. *He'd* been the one who'd suggested the reason she'd been so blackout drunk the night she was found in that boardroom was because she'd mixed her anxiety medication with alcohol. He'd made her believe the scandal he'd orchestrated had been all her fault, and she'd believed it.

The patrol car arrived at the Sheriff's Office. After she was ushered inside, she was told something about jurisdiction and departments and maybe they mentioned the Colorado Bureau of Investigation. It really all blurred together.

But what *did* crystallize in her brain, as the enormity of what Matt had done to her grew and grew... and as the betrayal seeped deep into her bones... was her fury.

A fury so complete and powerful, that she could not even consider the possibility that Matt could get away with any of this.

But hand in hand with that fury came fear. Matt's words played on repeat in her brain:

Never mention any of this to anyone. Never discuss what I've told you today, never discuss what happened at Curtis Pharmaceuticals.

Ever.

That means the cops.

I'll be right there, all the time.

I'll order the death of your dear Nanna. There'll be no warning. And after your Nanna it will be... maybe your pretty friend, Casey?

Matt had been so clear. She'd believe him then, and

she believed him now. One of his henchmen being dead and another in custody made no difference – there would always be more.

Andy had saved her today, but he couldn't protect her all the time, or her Nanna, or Casey.

I'll be right there, all the time

Matt would know something had happened to the boss and the brute when they couldn't be contacted. He'd be on high alert, just waiting for her to say something. Matt was an IT genius – if he didn't already have access to law enforcement databases she'd be stunned.

No, she realized. He wouldn't be waiting. He would already be making sure that if she did say something, there would be no evidence, and he would fabricate an alternative reality that utterly undermined anything she said. He'd done it before and he'd do it again. If she spoke, people would die... *and* Matt would remain free.

She couldn't allow that to happen.

She needed evidence before she spoke to the police. Irrefutable, undeletable, absolute evidence.

"Do you have any ideas why you were kidnapped, Ms Chapman?" the detective asked.

She took a deep breath. "No," she said, shaking her head. "No idea at all."

But the evidence she needed?

For that, yes. She did have an idea.

Andy didn't see Violet for hours.

He met remotely with Shadow Ops and a trusted,

very senior member of the Colorado Bureau of Investigation to provide a statement, and he was then free to go. Not that he was going anywhere without Violet.

Instead he sat in the Sheriff Office's waiting room, his knees bouncing impatiently, until Violet was finally done. She walked out with a couple of detectives around noon, her hair damp and combed back from her scrubbed-clean face. An impressive bruise stretched from her cheekbone to her temple.

Her eyes widened as he stood, but she smiled.

"You're still here?" she asked, her smile becoming a little unsure.

He frowned. "Of course."

A nod. "Do you mind giving me a lift back to Falcon?"

His frown deepened. "That's why I'm here."

"Oh," she said.

They walked outside to the parking lot in a bubble of awkward tension.

He paused with his hand on the passenger side door, just as he'd been about to open it for Violet.

"I'm sorry," he said gruffly. "For kissing you. It should never have happened."

"Hard disagree," she said blithely. "Can we talk in the car? I'd like to get back to Falcon as soon as we can so I can see my Nanna."

Then she reached for the door handle herself, and when her fingers brushed his knuckles, the instant electric sparks between them made him snatch his hand away. She looked up at him and rolled her eyes as she tugged the door open. "This is really silly," she said.

"It's really not," he argued, but she'd slammed the door shut behind her.

He jogged around the truck's bed and climbed into his own seat.

"It *is* silly," Violet persisted. "Whatever this is. It's silly, and stupid, and..." She paused. "Actually, you're right, it's not silly. It's disrespectful."

The truck spluttered to life. "I do agree with that," he said. "That's why I was at your house last night, to apologize."

Andy pulled out of the parking lot and onto the highway. It was about a two-hour drive back to Falcon, and the tension between them was thick with frustration.

"Apologize for what?"

"For manhandling you against your car."

She made a negative buzzer noise. "*Bzzzzttt.* Wrong answer."

"Pardon me?" He slanted a glance in her direction.

She gave a huff of exasperation. "I *liked* that. What I didn't like was your bullshit rejection after." Then she added. "And you did it again after our kiss. Not with words this time, but you rejected me in the walls you put up the moment the patrol cars arrived." He had to focus on the interstate, but he could see her knotting her fingers together on her lap in his peripheral vision. "And it's not fair. I've been honest with you. In the parking lot. Even, in a way, when I walked in on you after your shower in the break room. And I was definitely honest with you outside that cabin, and I'll continue to be, because Andy, I thought you were dead last night, and I could easily have ended up dead myself and, well..." She shook her head. "If I thought you weren't into me, I could accept that. But Andy, you literally risked your life to save me today. You told me how scared you were knowing I'd been kidnapped, then went full caveman and called me *yours*." She swallowed. "So, I call bullshit on all of this. On you apologizing for things I don't want you to apologize for, for saying that awesome kiss should never have happened, and for you not giving a shit about rejecting me – about hurting me - again, and again, and..." Her voice cracked. "...again."

The rusty truck's tires squealed as he hit the brakes and pulled over. They were on a twisty section of the interstate, and he came to a stop maybe 50 feet from the asphalt under the shade of a small group of trees.

In the abrupt silence after he cut the engine the sound of their breathing – hers soft, his harsh – was deafening.

"Violet," he said. "I'm so sorry. I'm an asshole."

"No, you're not," she said softly. "You're just acting like one. Why?"

He ran a hand through his hair, furious with himself for the hurt he'd caused Violet. Why hadn't he been able to keep his distance? Control himself?

He shook his head. "I don't talk about it," he said. Not to Natalie, or any of his girlfriends. Not anyone.

She kept her gaze forward, staring down the empty interstate. "Guess that tells me all I need to know then," she said.

"It just tells you there is some shit in my life I don't talk about," he said. "It has *nothing* to do with you, Violet. Honestly, Violet you are..." There was no other word for it. "...perfect. If there was any way I could make this work. If I could be the man that you deserve..."

"Oh stop," she said. "I don't need you to say pretty things to protect my ego. Of course it has everything to do with me. You want me, just not enough." She twisted on her seat to face him. "Thank you for saving me. For whatever reason. But you don't owe me an explanation for not wanting me more." She shrugged. "Just stop the bullshit though. Please? You've made your decision and that's the end of it."

"You're more than enough, Violet," Andy said, gripping the steering wheel he still held tightly. "You're everything."

She laughed dryly. "As I said, Andy, you've got to stop with this bullshit."

"Violet—"

But how could he explain? How could he possibly? There was so much that his decision was all wrapped up in – The Fox & Laughton, Natalie, his father. Cez. Where could he begin? How could he begin?

She held a hand up in a stopping motion. "It's okay. Can we just go home?"

None of this was okay. He hated this, all of it. But he nodded.

"Can I ask one question though?" she said quietly.

. . .

VIOLET FACED Andy across the truck's center console. He was gripping the steering wheel so tight his knuckles were white.

"Why will you fuck the women you meet when you fight, but not me?"

There it was. Her pride had officially hit rock bottom.

Internally she cringed in the heavy, weighted silence.

Was it her bone deep exhaustion that'd removed her ability to filter her thoughts and emotions around Andy?

No. With Andy it was *always* like this. Her emotions at the surface with no filter. Whether they were sparring at work, or the way she taunted him in the parking lot near The Roost.

She was doing it again, she knew. In the question itself but even in her crude choice of words. She was taunting him. Teasing him.

What did she want? To push him so hard that he rejected her so brutally she finally let go? Or to push him so hard he broke through the walls that he'd built between them?

Because she found it impossible to believe the man who'd risked his life to save her, who'd kissed her, and who'd held her against her Prius in a way that made her hot even now as she thought about it – could just walk away.

She needed him to say something now that *made* her believe none of that meant anything.

"Violet..."

Her name was a strangled groan on his lips.

Finally he let go of that damn steering wheel and

looked at her. His gaze was dark and raw as it raked up and down her body.

"No pretty words, Andy," she said firmly. "Just answer my question."

He held her gaze with his as he repeated it. "Why will I fuck the women I meet when I fight, but not you?" He shook his head. "That damn *fights, fucks and flees* gossipy shit is way out of control."

She took another deep breath. "Please, Andy. The question?"

He looked down as he ran both hands through his hair, leaving it disheveled. Then he looked up at her almost sheepishly. "There hasn't been any fucking or fleeing for ages, Vi," he said. "So, to answer your question – I'm not. I'm not fucking anyone."

She blinked at him, stunned. "Define *ages*."

His lips quirked upwards. "Since I met you."

She let out a breath in a *whoosh*.

"Wait," she said, totally discombobulated. "What does that mean?"

He raised an eyebrow. "You tell me," he said. "I only recently learned we're both in the same predicament."

The tension in the truck had shifted to something hot and electric. Something thick with anticipation.

She licked her lips. "For me," she said, her voice a husky tone she barely recognized. "It's because I don't want anyone else."

He shrugged. "Exactly."

"Oh no," she said firmly. "You don't get away with that. I need to hear it from you."

He held her gaze as she worried her bottom lip. "I don't want anyone but you, Violet," he said.

His words washed over her in a delicious shiver.

"Well," she said. "That's about the stupidest thing I've ever heard."

"You said it, too!" Andy replied, looking rather offended.

She laughed and slapped a hand to her chest. She laughed properly and uproariously for long minutes, while Andy just sat there looking increasingly bemused.

Finally her laughter slowed to hiccupping giggles, and she casually unclipped her seatbelt.

"What are you doing, Violet?" Andy asked cautiously.

She kicked off the flip-flops she'd been given at the Sheriff's Office and climbed onto her knees on the passenger seat before eyeing Andy across the center console.

"There seems a simple solution to the problem of two people who only want each other," she said, all matter of fact.

"Violet..."

She reached for the top bottom of her satin blouse. "I totally respect you have some private issues you aren't prepared to share that prevent us dating or whatever—"

"No, that's not it at all," he began. But he stopped as she slid open the top button of her blouse. Then the next.

"It isn't?" she said lightly. "Should I stop?" She let her expression become crestfallen. "Such a shame, as I really wanted to show you my new bra—"

But the rest of her sentence was lost in a shriek as he grabbed her around the waist and dragged her onto his lap.

Just like that, the atmosphere in the truck shifted from Violet's teasing and lightness to something almost predatory.

Violet gasped as Andy held her firm so she straddled his waist, then roughly rubbed her up and down the front of his jeans.

"Damnit, Violet," Andy groaned as he glared at her. His gaze was hot and hard, and his hands at her waist weren't gentle. "This isn't what you want."

Deliberately she rubbed herself against his hardness again, loving how his head fell backwards as he lost himself in the sensation. *I did that,* she thought. She did it again.

He groaned. "Violet...*fuck...*"

"This is what I want," she said, leaning forward to cradle his face in her hands. "I want this so bad."

But he held her still before she could rub herself against him again. "You were kidnapped less than 24 hours ago, Vi," he said firmly. "Are you sure you're thinking straight? Do you really want to fuck me on the side of the interstate in some shitty old truck?"

She held his gaze. "Yes." She traced his brows, then his cheekbones, with her fingertips. "It's been a year of wanting this, Andy. I don't want to wait any longer."

"But after?"

She shrugged. "This isn't about after. This is a solution to a problem we both share."

Right now, she genuinely couldn't care less about *anything* beyond this. Beyond what she wanted so desperately right now.

Andy.

His gaze was so hot it near scorched her skin. "You're sure," he said, but it was a statement. He sat up to press a hot kiss against her neck as he ground her against him with big hands at her hips. He pressed kisses and nips against her skin as he made his way to her ear. His tone when he murmured against her skin no longer held even the hint of a question. "You want my cock so bad you'll have it in broad daylight. When anyone could see," he said.

They were in the shadows a good distance from the asphalt, but he was right – they were in public. This was also, technically, against the law – and something she'd never, ever considered before.

She didn't care.

His hands bumped hers as they both clumsily unbuttoned her blouse.

"You don't care who sees what's mine?" he asked, as he pushed open the fabric. His next words were reverent. "Jesus H Christ," he breathed. "You are so damn beautiful."

"*Yours*," she said on a moan, and was rewarded with a desperate kiss.

Their lips and tongues met and clashed and it was imperfectly perfect as they both kissed each other like... well, like they'd waited forever for this.

His clever hands shoved down her bra cups to shape

her breasts, and his fingers quickly learned exactly how she liked her nipples touched. Then he pulled her up so his mouth could follow the same path as his fingers.

"Any cars driving by, smart girl?" he asked her, his breath hot against her tight nipple. "Can anyone see me making these mine? Making *you* mine?"

But then he sucked her into his mouth, and all she could see was stars. And the only noises she seemed capable of making were indistinct moans or his name on a sigh… or one single word: *yours. Yours. Yours. Yours.*

She plucked uselessly at his T-shirt in an ineffective effort to remove his clothing. Andy was, in contrast, far more effective at unbuttoning her jeans, and then her bra and shirt were gone.

But even Andy wasn't clever enough to get her skinny jeans off her while she straddled him, but he easily flipped her over so she sat on his lap. "Take these off," he said, a gravelly command she was more than happy to oblige.

Her jeans and emerald lace thong were enthusiastically discarded and then she was once again straddling Andy, now completely naked.

He kissed her in between his constant stream of praise.

So fucking hot. So damn beautiful. I always knew you were this perfect.

Usually Violet felt none of these things, but in the shade of these spruce trees her hips didn't feel too wide or her belly too round. She didn't feel too pale, or too tall. Instead, she was all the things that Andy said.

Including his favorite word: *Mine.*

I'm yours. I'm yours.

Their kisses became more urgent, his touch less about finesse and purely about pleasure. His fingers slid briefly through her folds as he kissed her jaw. "You're so fucking wet for me..." he breathed.

And then without preamble his thick finger was inside her, deep and firm, and she gave a gasp of pleasure. "More," she breathed.

He added another finger as she rode him desperately, her fingers searching for the snap to his jeans as his thumb pressed firm against her clit.

Then his jeans were undone and he was lifting his hips and her hand had found the shape of his cock. She pumped her hand up and down his length as his thumb at her clit made the heat in her belly grow tight and deliciously hot.

But he pushed her hand away. "Touch your breasts," he commanded. "Show me what you like."

Maybe if his clever fingers didn't already have her on the edge of pleasure, she would've felt self-conscious. Or maybe it didn't matter – because it was Andy.

So, with one hand at her breasts, playing with and pinching her nipples, the other at his shoulder to stop her collapsing in a puddle of sensation, and with his fingers inside her and his other hand at her hip moving her exactly the way he wanted... that *she* wanted... she came. She moaned his name as her forehead fell onto his shoulder as waves of sensation flooded her body.

As she caught her breath he grasped her hips with

both hands, pulling her forward up his thighs until his cock was at her entrance. But he held her firm when she went to move.

"No condom," he said against her ear.

"I have a rod in my arm," she replied. "And you already know I haven't been with anyone in a year."

He nodded. "I had a full medical only a couple of months ago for the Sha—" He stopped to kiss her, then murmured against her lips. "I'm clean."

And with that, she reached between them to grab his cock and guide him in, impatiently pushing herself onto him, unconcerned it had been so long for her and he was big and broad – she just wanted him inside her. She sucked in a breath as she was finally all full up, and she leaned forward to wrap her arms around his neck and kiss him, giving herself time to adjust and just simply to enjoy how this felt.

After all this time. After the sparring, the sparks and the tension... this was actually happening. It felt like a dream it was so good and so right.

"You okay?" His voice was a rumble as he kissed her neck. She realized his hands were trembling at her waist from his effort to remain still.

"Amazing," she said.

He smiled against her skin. "You absolutely are."

And then he lifted her up, and groaned. The pushed her down as he lifted his hips to meet her. She cried out as she ground against him, rocking her hips forward. Quickly they found a rhythm, his hands guiding her up and down, faster and faster. He grabbed her hand from his shoulder to guide it to her clit and she moaned as sparks flew and grew and tightened impossibly low in her belly.

"Oh my god...*Andy*," she said on a shriek as she came, pleasure exploding out from her core and in ripples throughout her body, all the way to the tips of her fingers and toes. A second later he yanked her down hard against his cock as he shouted her name into her hair, his huge body shaking in release as he dragged her into his arms and close against his chest.

They both remained silent but for the gradually quieting of their breathing as it returned to normal.

As Violet came back to herself, she became aware of the sweat on her skin, and the sensation of Andy's cock softening inside her. She became aware of her nakedness, and the stale smell of the rusty old truck. And when an eighteen-wheeler noisily drove by - while she was *almost* certain no one driving past could've seen what they'd just done - she was suddenly very aware of how exposed she was. She scrambled off Andy awkwardly and in silence he found a box of tissues in the glovebox as she awkwardly retrieved her underwear from where it'd been flung on the dash.

She tried to catch Andy's gaze so she could judge what on earth he was thinking. She had no idea what *she* was thinking, to be honest.

She regretted none of what they'd just done. It had been remarkable and everything that a year of foreplay (yes, she agreed with Casey now) promised.

But what now?

"Ready to go?" Andy asked, barely glancing at her.

She nodded. The truck coughed to life and gravel crunched beneath its wheels.

"Violet?" Andy asked a handful of minutes later.

But exhaustion had overcome her, and her eyes slid all the way closed as she leaned against the head rest.

"We need to talk," he said.

She mumbled something in agreement, but it was all she was capable of as she fell into a dreamless sleep. Whatever Andy had to say would have to wait.

SEVENTEEN

WITH VIOLET ASLEEP, ANDY USED THE LONG DRIVE to Falcon to organize all the shit in his head into some sort of coherent order.

Because he *had* to talk to Violet.

She was right, he'd been an asshole. She'd also been wrong – he hadn't just been acting like one. He was one. No question, for the way he'd treated her – let alone the reasons she didn't yet know about.

But despite that, despite his total assholery, she'd still wanted him. Wanted him enough to sit on his dick on the side of the highway...and *damn* it had been hot. Violet was amazing. But then, he'd always known that.

With her seated beside him, he itched to pull over again for round two. Or to drive her straight back to his place so he could lay her on his bed and kiss every last inch of her.

But none of that was going to happen – and not just because she'd fallen asleep minutes after he pulled onto the highway. What he needed to do was explain himself, and in doing so make her understand she didn't want anything to do with Andy Torres.

It was unacceptable that he'd allowed her to believe *she* was the issue. For her to believe the insanity that he didn't want her enough, when in reality he wanted her too much.

Mine.

He gripped the steering wheel tight.

Yours, she'd said.

Again, and again, and again.

When he finally came to a stop at her grandmother's house, he gently squeezed her shoulder to rouse her from her sleep.

"Violet," he said. "We're here."

She blinked up at him sleepily as she woke, rubbing at her eyes with one hand as she yawned.

"And we really need to talk," he continued. "Maybe after you've seen your grandmother?"

She nodded. "Yes," she said, covering her mouth as she yawned again.

But the slam of a screen door and the thud of feet on porch steps distracted them both. And not just one set of feet – there were many – as a large group of people streamed out of the house. Casey led the pack, jogging towards the truck, but remaining on the porch was the rest of the Shadow Team, Casey's mom, Cherry, the woman who ran the local lawn care business, a couple of coffee van regulars, and another half dozen people he didn't recognize.

"Violet!" she said, wrenching open the passenger side door.

Violet was embraced the moment she jumped out of the truck. Andy slid from his seat also, but gave the women some space – both had cheeks damp from tears.

"Why are all these people here?" Violet asked.

Casey tilted her head as she studied her friend with a curious expression. "Because you were *kidnapped*, Vi, and a lot of people were worried about you."

Violet frowned. "Even the rodeo committee are here," she said, shuffling her feet a little awkwardly. "I never expected this."

"You should've," Casey said simply. "Lots of people in Falcon care about you." But then she gripped Violet's hand and spoke carefully. "Violet, I don't want to alarm you, but your Nanna took a turn after she was told you'd been found safe and well. She's going to be just fine, but she's at the hospital in Glenwood Springs for observation for at least tonight."

"I need to go see her," Violet said immediately, her skin suddenly ashen.

"I'll take you now," Andy said.

Casey shook her head. "Nuh-uh," she said. "I heard how you were MacGyvering it across the state searching for Violet all night. You shouldn't be driving at all. Go sleep, and I'll take Vi to the hospital."

"But the police don't know why Violet was targeted," Andy said. "She may still be in danger."

Casey raised her eyebrows. "Why did they let you go home, then?" she asked Violet.

Violet shrugged. "It's okay," she said. "The two thugs who kidnapped me are either dead or in custody, I'm not worried."

"Dead?" Casey breathed. She looked at Andy. "Did you—?"

His nod was sharp. "It was unavoidable," he said. He stepped closer to Violet. "Vi, I don't want to scare you, but until we know what's going on, I think you *should* be on high alert."

"But Casey is right," she replied. "The cops let me go."

Only because the Shadow Team would be monitoring her 24/7, even if Violet and Casey didn't know it.

"I'll take you to the hospital," he repeated.

Casey shook her head. "And fall asleep at the wheel? No, Andy. I'll just take Dev with us. That big grump owes me one, anyway."

Andy resisted the urge to argue. He knew he shouldn't be driving, and Dev was as capable as he was of protecting Violet.

So, reluctantly, he nodded, and gestured for Dev to come over while Violet greeted her welcoming committee before heading inside to freshen up.

Andy called Shadow Ops for the latest intel from Dev's SUV. But there was nothing new to report – local law enforcement had seized the laptop that'd so urgently required its charger, but they were still no closer to understanding it's importance. Violet had provided no insight to detectives and the computer itself appeared brand new with nothing stored on it apart from the standard operation system. Shadow Ops had already provided briefs on both the kidnappers, and while their rap sheets painted a colorful criminal past, nothing linked either man to Violet. This wasn't surprising, as Andy had never thought either was the brains of this operation. But who was?

Andy ended the call none the wiser.

"Has Violet told you much about what happened in New York?" Dev asked. "Could her kidnapping be related?"

Andy shook his head. "From what the detectives told me, she's insistent she has no clue what this is about. Shadow Ops and the Colorado Bureau of Investigation is looking into any links back to her previous employer – a pharmaceutical company – but nothing is coming up so far."

"Are you sure she's told detectives everything she knows?" Dev asked.

"Have you met Violet?"

Dev laughed. "True, if she had anything to share with detectives, she'd probably find a way to express it in a spreadsheet to make her point."

"Her mother is another angle they're exploring," Andy explained. "A drug debt gone wrong is one theory. But I doubt it. Violet's mom's drug of choice nowadays is weed, she's buying off stoners not some vindictive drug lord."

"Could it have been random?"

It was possible, but it all felt far too elaborate. The remote cabin, the van with a satellite dish, and that laptop? Andy shook his head. "No, I'm certain she was their target."

He climbed out of Dev's truck as the women jogged down the front steps.

He touched Violet's arm and she stopped, looking up at him curiously. Casey went ahead to join Dev in his SUV.

"Call me when you leave the hospital," he said firmly. "I'll meet you here."

She nodded. Her gaze travelled from his eyes to his lips and back again, and she blushed.

"To talk?"

He nodded. "Be careful."

Her gaze slid away from his. "Of course."

"This is all a big over-reaction," Rose Chapman said in greeting as Violet rushed into her hospital room. "I was just a little light-headed with relief to hear you'd been found, is all."

Her Nanna was propped up in her bed, her complexion colorless and her pale-blue eyes rimmed in red.

As Violet hugged her gently, her Nanna wrapped her wiry arms around her. "Oh, honey, I was so frightened."

"Me, too."

"And to think they took you from our home," Rose continued. "I always felt safe in that house."

Violet stepped back as she mentally added something else to hate Matt for.

Her nanna shook her head. "I don't know how I'll ever sleep soundly there again."

"You will," Violet said firmly. *Once Matt is arrested and this is all over.*

"How?" Rose asked, but a nurse walked in, saving Violet from having to lie to her grandmother. It had been difficult enough lying to detectives, and thankfully she hadn't had to lie directly to Andy – as she wasn't sure she'd be any good at that, either. But what other choice did she have? She absolutely believed Matt's threats.

As the nurse spoke to her grandmother, Violet stepped into the hallway to make a couple of hot chocolates at a vending machine. Dev and Casey were waiting on a row of seats a little down the hall, and they both jumped to their feet for an update on her Nanna.

While she very much appreciated the ride to the hospital, Dev's bodyguarding was absolutely unnecessary – but how could she explain? *I know no one is going to kidnap me again because I know who is behind this but I can't tell you who as otherwise then I* would *need your protection – but not for me. For my Nanna, Casey, and everyone I care about.*

So no, she wasn't going to say a thing. About that, anyway.

"Nanna is doing fine," she said, as she punched the hot chocolate button on the machine. "Honestly, I can get an uber home. There's no need to hang around."

Dev was standing with his hands behind his back, his gaze sweeping up and down the hallway as she spoke.

His only reaction to her words was a raised eyebrow and a short response: "I'm staying."

Casey stepped closer, frowning. "How can you be so relaxed?" she asked. "Is this you in shock or something? You are way too chill, Vi. I'd be catatonic, honestly." Her frown deepened. "Are you sure you've been checked over?"

Violet nodded impatiently. "Yes, I'm fine," she said. "As I said, the police let me go, and the kidnappers are no longer a threat. That's it."

Dev grunted something indistinct.

She threw him a look. "Why are you and Andy so weird about this?" she said. "Why have you appointed yourself my bodyguards? You've left the military, there's no need for you to protect anyone."

"I'm staying," he repeated.

Violet rolled her eyes at Casey. "This is silly."

"Is it?" she asked quietly. "What's going on here, Violet? You're the most logical person I know. And logically, you should be pretty freaked out right now."

"I *am*," she said, honestly.

But to stop feeling like this, she needed Matt to no longer have any power over her. And to achieve that, she needed to get to New York.

Dev didn't let her out of his sight.

It was both infuriating and... nice.

Violet sat in the backseat of Dev's SUV and finally accepted she had no chance of getting to Denver – let alone

New York – today. When they arrived back in Falcon after the 30-mile journey from Glenwood Springs, Andy's truck was parked out the front of her place. And it was his truck, not the borrowed old red one. He was sprawled on one of the Adirondack chairs on the front porch, and she felt his gaze on her as she jumped down from Dev's SUV.

It was an unfamiliar sensation to have men looking out for her. The only men of her childhood were her mom's parade of boyfriends, and they'd been oblivious to her existence at best, creepy at worst. And once she'd moved in with her Nanna, it had just been them. She hadn't lived with any of her handful of boyfriends before Matt, and well, now she knew exactly how little he cared about her welfare.

But even as her heart warmed at the subtle nod that Andy gave Dev as she was silently handed over from one man's care to the other, she felt an almost equal resistance.

I don't need you to be my knight in shining armor.

That's what she'd told Andy the day she'd met him. Given she'd literally needed him to save her life only hours ago, it seemed a silly thing to think about right at this moment. She knew she was incredibly fortunate to now have men in her life that wanted to keep her safe. Still, she found herself feeling prickly after they'd both waved Dev and Casey goodbye.

"You didn't call me on your way back from the hospital," Andy said as she unlocked the front door.

She pushed the door open and threw a glance over

her shoulder as she stepped inside. "There was no need," she said. "I knew Dev was keeping you up-to-date of my every movement."

Yep, she definitely sounded prickly.

"You didn't like that?"

She walked through the house and into the kitchen at the rear. For the first time she noticed the brown paper take-out bags that Andy held as he placed them on the countertop. They were from Pho Sure, her favorite place to eat in Falcon.

"You bought me pho?" she said.

"Pho Tai," he said. "I think that's the one you like? I know you've had it for lunch at work a few times."

A few times was an understatement. "Thank you," she said, "that's really nice of you."

Andy laughed at her clipped tone. "Are you sure?"

"Yes," she said firmly. "Objectively it is extremely nice of you to bring my favorite dinner and insist on keeping me safe."

She reached for an overhead cupboard to grab a couple of wine glasses, then a bottle of rosé from the fridge. She held the bottle up in Andy's direction and he nodded before she poured them both a glass.

"I do realize I sound unhappy about it, and I also realize how stupid that is," she said.

She felt all fidgety so she remained standing as she took a sip of wine, propping her hip against the countertop. Andy remained standing too.

"You've had an intense twenty-four hours, Violet,"

Andy said, picking up his glass but not taking a drink. "You're allowed to feel however you feel."

She took another sip of her wine and looked at Andy across the rim of her glass. He'd changed and now wore a grey sweater and faded blue jeans. He was as handsome as always. *More* handsome now, as now when she looked at him there wasn't just an undercurrent of what *could be* between them. Now there was that, plus the heat of what they'd already done. She licked her lips at a sudden memory of how it'd felt to have his lush lips wrapped around her nipple. And of his uncompromising grip at her hips, manhandling her deliciously so she rode his cock *just right*.

His gaze dropped to her mouth and she had to close her eyes to re-route her thoughts to their conversation.

"I feel... unsettled," she said. "I'm not used to having anyone look out for me other than my Nanna. I'm very used to doing stuff on my own, and it isn't like I've had a choice in that."

"You don't need anyone to save you," he said. "You told me that the day we met."

She smiled. "I was remembering that conversation before, too. And that's just stupid in this situation, isn't it? Honestly, Andy, I've never been happier to see someone as I was when you walked into that bedroom in that godforsaken cabin. I *wanted* to be saved. Of course I did."

"But now you're feeling safe again it feels... claustrophobic?" he guessed.

She shook her head. "No. Unfamiliar. Or like clothing that's scratchy or doesn't fit. I also don't understand it, really. I mean – I work with you and Dev, why have you assigned yourself as my protectors?"

He frowned. "Because we care about you and you could still be in danger."

We care about you.

That was it, wasn't it? Having them care?

No one *ever* cared about Violet Chapman.

Not as a child in Falcon. Not as an adult in New York. Other than her Nanna, she could only rely upon herself.

Was that why she was restless? Or was it because Andy was here in her home, after what they'd done only hours ago?

She took another long sip of her wine as she studied Andy.

Should she tell him about Matt?

It was tempting. He could come with her to New York, and...

"*I* care about you, Violet," Andy said hoarsely. Then he cleared his throat as he gave a wry smile.

And just like that her focus shifted from Matt and New York, and she was mentally back in that shitty red truck, literally throwing herself at Andy even though he'd rejected her again, and again, and again. Yet the same man had risked his life to save her, and was here, now, determined to protect her. And the same man had made her come harder than she ever had before. Who hadn't wanted anyone but her, in a year.

It was as confusing as all hell. But she'd done enough talking. Now it was his turn.

She nodded.

He pushed his untouched wine glass towards the center of the marble countertop as he stepped towards her. He reached out as if to touch her face, then went still and shook his head.

"If I touch you, I'll forget all I need to say," he said.

She placed her own glass on the counter and waited.

He ran a hand through his hair, his gaze darting around the room. He was nervous, she realized, and it would've been adorable if she didn't care so much about what he had to say.

Because of course it'd been total bullshit when she'd told herself she didn't care beyond her desperate need to have Andy in that truck beside the highway. She wanted Andy just as much now. She wanted him more, in fact. But she wanted *all* of Andy. Not just the physical.

But she wouldn't allow him to hurt her again.

"I used to be a relationship guy," he said. "Maybe you already knew that, you knew I'd been engaged..." He ruffled his hair as he looked out the window. Outside the sky was turning all those nice purples and pinks of dusk. "But then something went down in the Middle East... and maybe you know this, too?"

She nodded. "A siege?"

"Yeah. I was there with another Delta Force operator – Tyler Cerra. Cez is what everyone calls him. We were at the hotel on R&R, and met Dev on our first day and – believe it or not – he used to be this pretty social dude. So, he'd collected a group of us from different units and we'd hang out a bit, sometimes eat together. That type of thing. Cez was having some wild nights, I was just drinking beer by the pool. It was pretty great, to be honest. Real nice place." He swallowed. "Then one morning during breakfast a terrorist group took control of the hotel. Some bombs went off. It was chaos, there'd been no hint there was any threat, but later on there was some speculation that the terrorists didn't like how the hotel was being so friendly with US troops."

He rested a hand on the counter top.

"The six of us, we did what we could. I have no doubt we saved a lot of innocent people, but when you're in that situation, making split-second decisions... sometimes you get it wrong. Dev... he's probably the most haunted by that. I made a call that saved a lot of people. He made a call and people died. And it wasn't because I made better decisions... it was luck. Damn luck, I think." His lips curved upwards. "Dev's a good guy," he said. "But the siege changed him."

He picked up his wine glass, looked at it, then put it down again. He then pushed away from the counter to pace the small kitchen.

"I'm not explaining this very well," he said.

"You're doing great," she said carefully, having the sense Andy was unearthing thoughts and ideas long buried.

He nodded. "Given my military career, maybe it's odd that the hotel is what changed me. I mean, death is part of war, and it was certainly part of my Delta Force assignments. The difference was, as an operator there was a purpose to what I was doing. And the deaths... they weren't innocent people. And certainly not so many of them." He rubbed at his eyes. "I think as well – as my "Delta Force Operator" self—" He drew the quotation marks in the air. "—I maybe felt separate to the reality of war. I was at work and still had my life at home. That was the life I was protecting. But in that hotel, everything blurred. I wasn't armed, I didn't have my team, except Cez. It was real life and it was brutal. And my life, for the first time, felt fragile."

He stopped his pacing to stand in front of Violet. She looked up at him, for the first time beginning to comprehend the reality of what Andy had done for a career. Safe here in Falcon, the special forces careers of the men she worked with had felt impressive but also... distant. Their physical strength was the only visible remnant of what they'd endured, and while she knew Sam worked hard to give the Cars & Coffee men time and space in their lives, she hadn't really thought about why that time and space was so necessary. She hadn't allowed herself to think about their trauma.

"I can't even imagine," she said quietly.

"Can't you?" he said. "Last night, when you were tied up in that van with those assholes, what did you care about?"

"My life and yours," she said.

"Exactly," he said. "Isn't that all we have? Our lives, and the lives of those we care about? It's all that matters. And when I came home from the Middle East, suddenly my life didn't fit. I'd had this vision of the life I wanted, but now it felt like just that – a vision. I was living in it but it didn't feel real."

He chuckled without humor. "I was going through the motions. Going on deployments, coming back home. I delayed my wedding to my fiancée. We were in this holding pattern for nearly two years, then I came home early to surprise Natalie – kind of like a last-ditch attempt to make an effort, and I found her in bed with Cez."

Violet sucked in a shocked breath.

Andy shrugged. "Cez and I, we'd drifted apart after the siege. I was too wrapped up in my own bullshit to notice Cez's, and he transferred teams a few months before I caught him with Natalie. Had been going on for a while, I gather. I never took the time to ask for the details."

"Oh, Andy—"

He held up a hand. "No," he said clearly. "I don't deserve any sympathy. I'd checked out of that relationship, yet when I found Cez with Natalie I..." He rubbed at his eyes again. "I lost it, Violet. I dragged Cez out of that bed and hit him hard enough to break his nose before I realized he wasn't doing a thing to stop me. But I didn't like that, so I punched the dry wall instead. Stuck my boot through a door. Made a fucking mess of my own apartment while the woman I thought I loved cried in a pile of blankets."

He gripped the countertop to look out into the backyard.

She took a step towards him but he shook his head. "Violet, here's the thing. I don't hit people outside of my job. I don't deliberately frighten women. You know why? Because my deadbeat dad terrorized my mom and I'd vowed never to be like him. Yet I did both of those things, and *I didn't want to stop.* I was so angry, and I don't even think I was just angry at Natalie or Cez. I was just angry. I was a fucking furious violent piece of shit, just like my dear old dad."

"Did you hurt Natalie?" Violet asked.

Andy's gaze swung back to meet hers directly. "No."

"Did you threaten her? Did she ever believe you would hurt her?"

"Absolutely not," he said. He narrowed his gaze. "But it wasn't just that day, Violet. I'd changed. Whenever I felt any sort of emotion, I wanted to get physical. I wanted to use my fists. I wanted to use my strength."

"That's why you box."

He nodded. "Yeah. I never used to be like this. And it's not just boxing. It's with women, too. I never used to be this guy – the guy who liked to use my strength when I have sex." His chuckle was flat. "I don't even have sex anymore. It's fucking. Now I like it fast, and a little rough. No emotion. I like to pick woman up, have them against a wall, or bent over a table."

"Or your hand over her mouth."

"No," he said. "That was a first, with you. With you, Violet... it's even more. I'm a damn caveman with you. All that possessive shit... calling you mine. It's messed up."

"Is it?" she asked softly.

His eyes widened. "Pardon me?"

"Haven't you been listening to me? I liked it when

you put your hand over my mouth. I really like it when you call me yours."

He shook his head. "No, it's controlling and aggressive and disrespectful."

"It could be," she conceded. "It's not something I've had a guy say to me before, and I'm certain I wouldn't like it with some men. Most men, probably." She grinned. "I'm fiercely independent, remember?"

It was a contradiction, and she sensed they were both considering this as they stood together in the kitchen, the light slowly fading as she absorbed what Andy had told her and how it made her feel.

"What do you mean," she said, "when you call me yours?"

His gaze instantly raked up and down her body.

She closed her eyes as she shivered beneath the force of his attention. Her eyes still closed she asked, "Yours to..."

He didn't say a word, but had he stepped closer?

"...touch?" she breathed. "Kiss?"

His breathing had become ragged.

"Hold? Lick?" Her eyes popped open as she sensed him step forward. She looked up to hold his gaze. His eyes were dark with heat and his own conflict.

He groaned. "Violet..."

"Or," she said, "do you mean, *yours to...* control?"

His eyes widened in shock. "*No.*"

"Force?"

"Violet, what are you—"

"Judge? Berate?"

"Christ no, of course not. Never."

She smiled up at his handsome, horrified expression as she reached for him, sliding her hand up the muscular shape of his arm and bicep. "Then I think we're good," she said. "Although maybe I'll just confirm." She slid a finger down his jaw, then rubbed her thumb across his bottom lip. He just stood there as if captivated. The sense of power she felt was in direct opposition to all that he'd said to her, all that he seemed to fear. "I'm yours, Andy Torres, to..." she chewed on her lip as his gaze became impossibly dark. "...claim..." she said in a husky tone she barely recognized. "...to fuck..." she breathed, as he bit gently down on her thumb. She reached her other hand to his cheek as she tried to tug him down to her mouth. "Yours to...fill."

It was as if something snapped inside Andy, as suddenly she was moving and flung effortlessly over his shoulder.

He headed up the stairs.

"Where's your room?" he asked as they reached the top. But she didn't need to reply as he located it close to the landing, strode inside and tossed her onto the bed. She bounced against her white quilt as she gasped in surprise, her glasses dislodging. "Andy—"

But then he was looming over her, his large body crawling across the bed until he'd framed her face with his hands.

"You deserve better than this," he said, as he pressed rough kisses against her jaw. "That siege, and what came after... it changed me. Broke me. You don't want this."

She tangled her fingers in his hair to drag his lips to her mouth. "Yes, I do," she said against his lips, then kissed him before he could argue again.

She didn't fool herself that they'd resolved much of anything, but what he'd shared felt like a gift – but his trust came with an insight into his torment, and his pain made her heart twist. She kissed him again and again, as if that would convince him he wasn't the broken, violent man he seemed so certain he was, or could be.

Andy's hands were moving, pushing up her t-shirt and sweater, then he sat up to pull both over her head. Her bra followed a moment later, then her jeans and panties.

He knelt, fully clothed between her legs, sliding his hands from her ankle to her knees to spread her legs wide apart.

"Mine," he said, his gaze on her pussy.

"Yours," she agreed.

And then his mouth was between her legs, his hands firm on her thighs as he kept her legs spread as his tongue licked up through her folds, tasting how drenched she was before locating her clit and circling it firmly.

Her back arched as she cried out, her hands flying backwards to grab onto the brass rails of her headboard. She held on tight as he explored her, his beard a delicious abrasion as his clever tongue determined exactly how she liked to be touched and tasted.

Her orgasm came fast and hard, his name a shriek on her lips: "Andy, yes, *God*, yours...Andy..."

She was still lost in a tide of sensation when she felt

his cock against her still wide spread thighs. She lifted heavy, sated eyelids to look at Andy – and watch as he tugged off his T-Shirt to reveal his heavily muscled torso, and the tattoos that made him even more beautiful.

He'd lost his jeans as well, so he was finally naked before her, and his expression was hot and determined. Casually he hooked one of her ankles onto his shoulders, then the other, pushing his body forward until his cock was right before where she was open and wet for him.

"Andy—"

He held her gaze as he gripped his dick to guide it to her entrance. Then he groaned one single word as he pushed all the way inside her in one, strong, stroke. "*Mine.*"

She cried out again at the delicious invasion of her body, then held on tight to her headboard as Andy pulled out almost all the way, before shoving himself back in. She was slick and tingly with aftershocks, and every powerful movement of his body triggered sparks and heat and electricity. It was a raw and primal coming together, as he took her… as he claimed her… and she loved it.

It was overwhelming in its intensity and *he* was remarkable in his power.

But all of that power was being used as much for her pleasure as his, as he tilted her hips and changed his angles to elicit gasps of pleasure that only grew louder and stronger as he found just the right angle to hit somewhere deep inside that triggered bursts of sensation that were almost too much for her to handle.

Then as he continued to plunge and pound, he fell

forward to capture her mouth, and to slide a hand between them so he could press his thumb against her clit.

And as they kissed and as he fucked her with unrelenting, utterly perfect strokes, she came, wrenching her mouth from his as she screamed his name and as the world went still as an explosion of pleasure consumed her body.

His own cry of completion was hoarse and deep against her ear, and his weight as he collapsed upon her was heavy and absolutely wonderful. She wrapped her arms around him, loving his weight and warmth, and the scent of sex and clean sweat.

He kept her in his arms as he rolled to his side, tucking her head beneath his chin.

"Violet..." he began.

"Later," she said firmly. "We can talk more later."

For now, they slept.

EIGHTEEN

The first time Andy woke it was to the sound of Violet entering her bedroom carrying a tray.

"I've heated up the pho," she said.

Vietnamese noodle soup was not an ideal meal for dinner in bed, so they followed up the meal with a shower, where Andy helpfully ensured that not one drip of soup remained anywhere on Violet's gorgeous skin, as he thoroughly explored her curves with his hands, a cloth, and his tongue.

When she wrapped herself in a pink towel and grabbed his hand to lead him back to the bedroom, any thoughts he may have had that they should talk, evaporated.

This time their coming together was slower, without the desperation of in the truck, or the first time on this bed. But that didn't mean he'd wanted Violet any less. In fact, as he traced her eyebrows with his fingertips, and kissed the freckles that dusted her nose, the depth of his need for her was all consuming. As she moaned and arched beneath him, he lost himself in her heat and the embrace of her arms and legs, and it seemed impossible that how good this felt could be something he could ever let go.

Mine.

But she wasn't, of course.

VIOLET SPENT FAR TOO much time laying in her bed watching Andy sleep.

She'd re-decorated her room since she'd moved back to Falcon – she'd bought a queen-sized bed, pulled down her old Robert Pattinson posters, and bought a small mountain of jewel-colored velvet cushions and throws to brighten up the off-white décor. But it was still very much her childhood bedroom, and she felt maybe it should be odd to have this huge, naked man sprawled beside her? Because despite her inherited reputation, she'd never had a guy in here before.

But it didn't feel odd.

It felt...really good. It would be so easy to fall asleep beside Andy and bask in how safe and secure it made her feel to have him near.

It would also be easy to wake him and tell him her plan.

Laying here in the darkness beside this man so determined to protect her, she questioned and re-questioned her decision.

But if she told him, then what? What could he actually do to help? He wasn't a cop, and he'd been retired from the military for years.

And telling him about Matt... would that put Andy in danger? Or her Nanna? Casey?

In the moonlight her gaze scanned her ceiling, then landed on her phone beside her bed. Had Matt bugged her phone? Her house?

The idea was ludicrous. Paranoid, probably.

But when she looked at the sleeping man beside her, or she thought about her helpless grandmother in Glenwood Springs, she just couldn't take the risk.

After all, she knew exactly how far Matt would go to protect his interests. He'd effortlessly destroyed her life, and he'd just as effortlessly order the murder of those she loved.

Love.

She let the word bounce about in her brain as she watched the rise and fall of Andy's naked chest.

Love, in the context of whatever this was they were doing, was equally as ludicrous as her concern that Matt was eavesdropping on her every conversation.

Wasn't it?

Oh, she *liked* Andy. She wanted him. In her bed, in her life.

She wanted him despite all he'd said in his attempt to scare her away. She wanted him *more* because of it, greedy for greater insight into the man who'd plagued her dreams and fantasies for twelve long months. Greater insight into why he'd so cruelly pushed her away... and would likely do so again.

Because he would, she thought. Unless he was prepared to fight his demons – the demons he carried from his abusive father, his military career, the siege, and the betrayal of his fiancée and best friend.

Unless he was prepared to fight his demons *for her*.

She slid to the side of the bed, gently lowering her bare feet to the floor. She flexed her soles against the nubbly texture of the chunky colorful rug beneath her bed.

Or... was this about her own demons?

Was her certainty he would ultimately reject her based on reality, or a lifetime of experience? Weren't they both the same thing?

She pushed herself to her feet, naked, shivering not from cold but from her discomforting thoughts.

I can't tell Andy the truth because it would put him in danger.

Was that the only reason?

Silently she collected her discarded clothing from where she'd piled it on her dresser.

Andy rolled from his side and onto his belly, one hand curled above his head. He was oblivious as she tugged on her underwear and jeans.

I don't need you to be my knight in shining armor.

That was it, wasn't it? In her youth, she'd carried unearned shame. As an adult, Matt had manipulated her worst fears to shame her again.

No one had believed in her in New York. As a teenager, no one had believed in her in Falcon.

Her whole life she'd had to fight to prove herself. She'd never just simply been *enough.*

Even the man who slept in her bed kept pushing her away. Would he even be here if she hadn't thrown herself at him?

Would he even be in this bed in the morning, if she did crawl back beside him? Or would his inevitable rejection come before dawn? Before she woke and had any chance to tell him the saga of Matt, and Curtis Pharmaceuticals, and infinitesimal data discrepancies that equated to millions?

She had no way of knowing.

But what she *did* know, she realized, as she straightened her shoulders and turned her back on her bed, was clear:

She had to do this herself.

THE SECOND TIME Andy woke up, Violet was gone.

NINETEEN

Violet caught the 6am flight to New York from Denver International.

She hadn't brought much with her, just her purse and her cell phone. She sat on the subway from JFK, staring blankly out the window as she tried to work out what to do.

Matt had "thrown" her out of their shared apartment the same day she'd been discovered naked in that boardroom. Her jaw was tense as she remembered what she now knew as his false outrage and hurt. His fury at her "betrayal".

It had all been so convincing. He'd refused to listen to a word of her explanation, or her insistence that she couldn't remember anything, and that it must all be some terrible mistake.

But the reality had been she'd never thought it was a mistake. She'd all too easily believed she was capable of such appalling behavior. That the scandal had simply exposed her true self, and the accomplished version of Violet Chapman that had come before was the imposter.

That day had been chaotic. She'd been instantly dismissed at Curtis Pharmaceuticals, then had tearily confessed to Matt in the narrow galley kitchen of their Midtown apartment. He'd demanded she leave immediately, berating her as she swiftly packed a suitcase of clothing, never leaving her side. He'd demanded her key and she'd handed it over, overwhelmed with guilt.

She'd stayed in a hotel at first, later renting short term accommodation and returning to Matt's apartment for her belongings. He'd hovered over her, but hadn't helped at all, and it was only later she'd realized she'd left random things behind – a winter coat in a closet, a shoebox full of UChicago memorabilia, that type of thing.

She got off the subway at 50th Street Station, then walked the couple of blocks to her old apartment block on 52nd Street. She wore her sunglasses and a baseball cap because she knew Matt's weekend routine well – sleep in, then head out for a lunch of hot pastrami on rye at the sandwich shop near the Chrysler Building on 3rd Avenue. Matt *never* ate at home, and while she supposed it was possible he'd shaken up his routine since she'd left New York, she doubted it. It was just after noon, and the last thing she wanted was to bump into Matt on his way for his regular Sunday sandwich.

There was a Starbucks diagonally across from Matt's tall, red brick apartment building. Violet ordered an almond milk latte and sat in one of the window booths, her focus on the apartment's lobby.

Come on Matt, leave.

She'd drained her latte with no sign of Matt, all the time absolutely aware that Matt might already have left. But if he had – she'd just wait for him to return, then wait some more until he left again for dinner.

She needed to be sure his apartment was empty.

She'd just returned to her booth with a cinnamon bagel – more to justify her extended use of the booth than because she could stomach eating anything – when Matt walked out onto the sidewalk.

She slid across the vinyl seat away from the window as she watched him head – predictably – east for the mile-long walk to his favorite sandwich. As she watched him walk, utterly unaware of her eyes on his back, her heart beat in anticipation and her shoulders tensed in anger and frustration.

To see Matt walking so carefree, so content in his life, given what he'd done to her... and what he'd threatened... her fury didn't bubble beneath the surface, it was a full-on rolling boil.

You asshole.

You total, fucking asshole.

She left her bagel untouched on the tabletop.

You're not getting away with anything.

WHERE WAS SHE?

He'd slept in. Andy *never* slept much past dawn, but

today he had. A combination of a severe lack of sleep combined with bone deep... satisfaction? Contentment?

Andy wasn't sure, but he did know he couldn't remember the last time he'd slept so well, or woke feeling so rested.

That sensation didn't last long.

He'd stretched and rolled towards Violet's side of the bed as sun streamed through narrow gaps in the blinds. She wasn't there. Instead, a torn-out piece of notepaper lay on her pillow.

I HAVEN'T BEEN KIDNAPPED AGAIN, I promise.

I'll be back soon – tonight or maybe tomorrow. Please don't worry.

Violet

HE STARED MUTELY at Violet's familiar neat handwriting as his gut plummeted.

Oh no. Oh *fuck*.

He was out of bed, yanking up his jeans as he scrambled to work out where she'd gone, and *why*. T-Shirt bunched up in his hand he grabbed his cell from the back pocket of his jeans and called her while he twisted the blinds open all the way to check for her Prius on the driveway. It was gone. His call went immediately to voicemail.

Where was she?

The next call he made was to Shadow Operations.

The voice on the other end of the call was infuriatingly calm as he was asked question after question: *When did you last see her? What clothing is she wearing? Any idea as to where she may have gone? Who she may contact?*

But the last time he'd seen her was at around 2am when he'd dragged her into his arms, her bare back to his chest, her thick auburn hair tickling his nose and chin. That was literally all he knew.

As he hung up the phone to leave Shadow Ops Intel to work their magic, Andy was absolutely certain of one thing: Violet may not have been kidnapped this time, but wherever she'd gone now was linked to her kidnapping.

He could think of no other reason for the secrecy of her disappearance. She knew he was concerned for her safety, even if she'd resisted his protection – yet she'd left without a word.

He ran a hand through his hair. *Why hadn't she trusted him?*

He tugged on his T-Shirt, then sat on the edge of the bed to pull on his socks and boots.

He leaned forward, his forearm on his knees and his head in his hands. Surely she must know, after he'd raced through the night and into the mountains to find her, that she could trust him? That he would do fucking *anything* to protect her?

He scrubbed his fingers through his hair. *Fuck.* How had he let her out of his sight?

He stood up abruptly and ran down the stairs, willing Shadow Ops to call him back with a lead – any lead.

Out on the porch he paced as he waited, the keys to the truck gripped tightly in one hand, trying to tamp down his panic.

Yesterday he'd been so certain Violet had told the police everything she knew, because Violet was the most honest, by the book person he knew. She loved creating guidelines and governance models – she'd transformed Cars & Coffee and the Falcon Rodeo Committee. She loved data, facts and making decisions based on evidence – as he'd learned with their coffee cup supplier saga. And she was honest outside of work too – amazingly, incredibly honest. She hadn't shied away from telling him how she felt, or calling him on his bullshit.

Yet she'd likely lied to the detectives, and lied by omission to him. There was only one logical explanation as to why she would do that.

She'd had to.

Or at least, she'd believed she'd had to.

His cell phone rang.

He barely let the Shadow Ops Intel Officer finish their greeting before speaking, his words low and gruff. "Where is she?"

"Karl!" Violet said with determined brightness as she crossed the marble floor of the lobby at Matt's apartment building to approach the sharply dressed doorman behind the front desk.

Karl's eyes lit up as he recognized her. "Ms Chapman!" he said with his clipped British accent. "What a pleasure to see you and your lovely smile once again, I heard you moved home to Colorado."

"That's right!" she said, her cheeks aching from the effort to fake a breezy demeanour. "I'm only in New York for the weekend, but I organized with Matt to pick up a few things I accidentally left in the apartment when I moved out."

Karl nodded as if he hadn't once carried her hastily packed suitcase and flagged a yellow cab while she'd desperately swiped at devastated tears she hadn't been able to stop. "Mr McKendrick has just popped out," Karl said apologetically. "Would you like to leave a message? Or wait for him to return?"

"Oh!" she said, feigning annoyance. "He told me he'd be here." She frowned. "I'm meeting a friend for lunch, I really don't have time to wait." She huffed out a sigh and chewed on her bottom lip, *really* hoping she wasn't over-doing this. "Is there any chance you could let me in? I just want to grab a coat and a couple of other bits and bobs. Matt does know I'm coming."

Karl drummed his fingers on the polished oak countertop of the concierge desk. "I really shouldn't, Ms Chapman," he said. "Maybe it would be best if you organized another time with Mr McKendrick."

She had expected this. Karl was a good doorman, but she didn't feel bad about what she needed to do next.

"I don't have another time," she said, her voice now wobbly. "I fly back to Denver later this afternoon." She shook her head. "Karl, I just need a couple of minutes in the apartment now. It's taken me all this time to build up the courage to come back here, and I..." Her voice cracked, and her reedy desperation was definitely not false. "Please. I just want to get my stuff and move on."

She rubbed at her eyes as if she were crying as she held her breath.

Please, Karl.

He drummed his fingers one more time.

She sniffed, and reached for a tissue from the box on the countertop.

Karl sighed, then nodded. "Okay." She let out a relieved breath as the doorman bent down to unlock the safe that stored spare apartment keys. "I still use that budget spreadsheet you made for Cynthia and I," he said, as he handed over the key. "It was so kind of you to teach us how to use it."

"I'll be quick," she said, with total honesty. "Thank you."

It only took a minute or two to take the elevator to the twelfth floor and jog across the patterned carpet to what was once her own front door. She dropped the key the first time she tried to unlock it, as her heart fluttered against her ribs.

Door open, she took the handful of steps to the built-in closet as the heavy apartment door clicked shut behind her. She twisted the handle and held her breath as she yanked the closet door open.

The little Japanese tapas bar in the NoMad district, about a twenty-minute ride on the subway from their apartment, had the best vegetable tempura Violet had ever tasted.

Matt studied her as she took a bite of a perfectly battered slice of sweet potato.

"You look extremely pleased with yourself," he said.

She grinned. They sat side by side on barstools, each with a cocktail, and then a half dozen bowls of delicious food to share before them. "I had a great day at work," she said.

He raised his pale blond brows in question.

"I found something interesting in one of my new dashboards," she said. "You know how I've connected a few new data sources? I'm pretty sure I've told you about it before." Violet knew she'd told Matt, but his eyes had a tendency to glaze over when she got a little too excited about data. "It took me a couple of hours to be certain, but I've found something really interesting. I don't know what's caused it yet, but I've found a mismatch somewhere between Curtis's income statements and what's recorded in the ledger. I did a few calculations, and while the discrepancies are tiny at an individual level, the volume of transactions we're dealing with make it really add up." Matt was focusing on his chicken skin skewer. She glared at him. "Matt, are you listening?"

"Dashboard. Sources. Mismatch," he said, not looking up. "See?"

Violet frowned. "I'm really excited about this," she said.

His laugh was smug. "Babe, no one gets excited about data other than you."

"The Curtis Senior Execs will be pretty excited when I tell them tomorrow," she said.

Matt coughed on his chicken skewer, and she maybe thumped him on the back a little more enthusiastically than necessary as he spluttered into a napkin. Why did Matt do this? She felt like she literally spent half her life listening to Matt talk about stuff he found interesting – everything from his tropical fish to his favourite topic – how he was going to spend all his money once he was wealthy. How *he was going to achieve that was less clear. They both had well-paying jobs, but this was New York.*

But listen to her very occasionally ramble on about her *job? He'd just tune out.*

It was infuriating.

Coughing fit over, Matt dabbed at his lips and twisted in his chair to make a bit of a show of giving Violet his full attention. "Here," he said. "I'm ready to be fascinated by your adventures in data today."

But he'd ruined it. She shook her head. "It's okay."

She shoved her hand into the pocket of her checked wool coat to grip the USB flash drive she'd brought home with her from work. She'd left her work laptop in the office as it was running several overnight calculation jobs, but she'd planned to play with an extract of the data on her personal computer after dinner, and maybe show Matt, if he was interested.

Ha! She should've expected this response.

She left the flash drive in her pocket as she sipped her Japanese gin cocktail. Matt polished off a chicken skin skewer before throwing a grin in her direction.

"I'm sorry, babe," he said. "But I'm sure your Senior Execs will be suitably impressed tomorrow."

"They will be," she said.

THE COAT WASN'T THERE.

Violet shoved each of Matt's coats and rain jackets to one side of the small closet, then moved them to the other one by one, just to be certain.

But there was no mistake. The familiar grey and black check of her one-time favourite coat was nowhere to be seen.

Logically, she'd known this was a possibility. Matt could've taken it to Goodwill anytime in the last year. But this was *Matt*. He didn't even use this closet. It was full of expensive ski gear he'd used exactly once and a collection of umbrellas – including a vibrant sunflower print umbrella that was hers. She grabbed it.

I'm at least taking this with me.

She laughed a little hysterically. She had an umbrella and no flash drive. No evidence. At the time she'd never thought to check the files on the flash drive, because when her "errors" had been identified, she'd confirmed them herself with the live data. It had never occurred to her that the data had been doctored. It had been all too easy to believe she'd been wrong, and for her self-belief to falter.

She closed the closet, trying to *think*.

She didn't have much time. Karl would come looking for her, or Matt could return.

The apartment had a narrow hall, then opened up into an open plan lounge and kitchen area, with two bedrooms off the side. One was Matt's study.

She ran in there, tugging open the top drawer of his desk where she knew Matt kept a small mountain of flash drives, just in case hers was there. It wasn't. Even if it was, Matt would've checked the contents. *This is a waste of time.*

She eyed his laptop. Could she log in?

She dismissed the idea as she took several deep breaths as she fought back panic. Unlike her, Matt did not reuse passwords. She had no chance of guessing his login. She randomly opened the desk drawers and scanned the room... looking for what? A file labelled: *Evidence*?

Umbrella in hand she headed for his bedroom. There was a small walk-in closet that had once been half Matt's and half hers. Now his clothing filled the entire space, with dirty clothes in a pile in a corner.

She scanned the space. Was her coat in here?

Her eyes landed on a familiar box on the shelf above the hanging clothes. It was her box of memorabilia, an old shoebox with a UChicago sticker on the end. She stood on tip toes to try to grab it, but couldn't reach. She used the umbrella to nudged it closer to the edge of the shelf, then jumped and grabbed at it, dislodging it slightly. She ducked as something on top fell to the carpet.

A framed photograph of her and Matt on holiday in Miami. It had once been on her nightstand, but she'd left it behind. Matt had put it here. Was there more of her stuff up on the shelf?

She dragged a duffel bag over to stand on as she reached blindly upwards. She yanked down the UChicago box, and dropped it carelessly onto the floor, its contents scattering. Next came a photobook she'd made on their one-year anniversary, then her fingers touched fabric.

Her coat?

She jumped on the lumpy duffle bag, her fingertips gripping the fabric just enough to tug it forward. She yanked hard, but over balanced, stumbling off the duffle bag. As she fell the coat – *and it was* the *coat* – landed on top of the mess of UChicago miscellanea as she landed on her butt with a thud. A UChicago bottle opener dug into her palm as she pushed herself off the carpet.

"I've always felt that you really overdid it at the UChicago Spirit Shop."

The low, quiet voice was utterly relaxed.

"Matt!" she squeaked, stumbling again as she tried to stand, falling on top of the pile of stuff in her panic. There was a crack when she stepped on the photo frame as she scrambled to her feet, taking a couple of tries to get her balance.

She scuttled back as Matt stepped into the room and calmly picked the frame off the closet floor. He shook his head.

"We had fun together, didn't we, Violet?" he asked in a conversational tone. "So sentimental of me to keep your stuff. I had thought to send it to you, but I was supposed to hate you for what you did." He shrugged. "It was all rather complicated."

"Not really," she said. "You being an asshole is very clearcut."

He gave a bark of surprised laughter. "Oh Violet," he said, "you always have been bold. Is that why you're here?"

He took a step forward.

It was a New York closet, so that put him very close. Matt was shorter and far rangier than Andy, but he'd still easily have 35 pounds on her. What were her options here? Run? Scream?

Her heart hammered against her ribs.

"What are you searching for, babe?" Matt said as he stepped even closer, kicking the coat and umbrella aside. "Because this isn't about your UChicago travel mug, is it?" He grinned, his gaze travelling up and down her body. "Or did you just miss me?" he asked in a mocking tone. "Want to get back together, ride on the coattails of my genius?"

"I hate you," she said, succinctly.

His grin fell away and his eyes hardened. "You never did comprehend my brilliance, did you? Thought you were so clever, so secure in your pre-ordained journey to Executive Vice President."

"You were jealous of me," she said, suddenly comprehending. "That was part of it, wasn't it? Protecting your crime, but also tearing me down in the process. You're as bad as some of the people I grew up with, couldn't deal with me pushing past what *you* determined I should be."

"Oh, Violet," he said, shaking his head. "You aren't pushing past anything anymore. You're right where you *should* be. Where you deserve. Small town nowhere, USA."

Her smile was broad. "Falcon is *exactly* where I want to be," she said, realizing as she said it that it was true. "But there are no *shoulds* about it. I decide what I want, now."

She wasn't controlled by the opinions or expectations of others. *When had that happened?*

"Brave words given your situation," Matt said dismissively.

And he was right. Trapped in a closet with a man who she knew was capable of at the very least ordering violence was not the time for self-reflection. But was he capable of violence himself? He held the photo of them in his hand, but no weapon.

"*Why are you here, Violet?*" Matt asked, reaching out to grab her upper arms. He gave her a shake, and her head bumped against the shoe rack behind her. "*What did I forget?*"

Suddenly she could see the doubt in his gaze. Despite all he'd told her, of his brilliance, of all the clever ways he'd protected his code, and the trail back to himself, he was threatened by her. He'd told her there was no way for anyone to prove what he'd done, for anyone to tie him to his crimes.

Yet he'd panicked and kidnapped her when she'd done something as benign as contact a software helpdesk – which was hardly the covert actions of a woman working to uncover a dastardly crime. And he was panicking now.

What a pathetic, insecure, piece of scum he was.

She tried to shake his hands free, but he gripped tighter.

Her reaction was instinctive. There was no more strategizing her escape – she just fought. She kicked, her sneakered foot bouncing off his shin. She angled her knee towards his groin as he swore at her, but while she didn't make direct contact, he loosened his grip as he bent forward to protect himself. She rammed her shoulder against his chest as she pushed past him.

"You bitch!" he shouted, as she tried to navigate all the stuff on the floor. He grabbed at her ankle and she fell, narrowly missing the closet's doorframe as she threw her arms out to break her fall. Her glasses bounced out into the bedroom. She kicked out, but he didn't let go, looming over her from behind as she tried to crawl away. She gasped as he dropped his full weight on top of her, then grabbed her wrists and tugged them behind her back. She tried to wiggle and twist away, but it was no use – in moments he'd knotted something around her wrists. Then he held her ankles firm even as she kicked, tying them together too. Then he rolled her over, so she sat on the floor as he stood above her. She tested the business ties he'd used to secure her, but they held firm.

He put his hands on his hips as he gasped with exertion. Then he spotted something on the carpet between them.

"Is *this* what you were after?" he crowed, reaching down. He held the object up like a trophy.

She couldn't believe it. It must have fallen out as they'd struggled.

A flash drive.

TWENTY

ANDY HAD BOARDED HIS FLIGHT WITH NOTHING more to go on than what Shadow Ops had discovered: Violet had flown to New York early this morning.

That was it.

At this stage there are no links between Violet's kidnapping or kidnappers and her connections in New York, the Shadow Ops Intel officer had told him. *We'll keep searching. But are you certain she's in danger?*

He had no idea how he'd been able to answer that question with something resembling civility, when all he'd wanted to do was shout obscenities down the phone. *Don't you understand? Violet would fucking never...*

But that was the thing, wasn't it? What he was realizing? He *did* know Violet. He knew, right now, deep in his soul, that something was very, very wrong. And this wasn't even the intuition that'd led him the right way during the hotel siege, or turned him around when he'd headed too far down the interstate. It was something different. Something more, and something he definitely didn't have the capacity to unravel as he used every technique he knew to hold himself together – when even in a war zone he'd never felt so close to falling apart.

By the time he'd landed four hours later every muscle in his body was tense with dread. Violet's phone was still switched off, and he had nothing more from Shadow Ops than a list of locations she'd been known to frequent when she'd lived in New York: her old apartment, her place of employment, a yoga studio on East 51st Street – and so on.

It was fuck all to work with.

Where are you, Violet?

He'd had nothing to go on but gut instinct. And his gut – and his life experience – told him the greatest danger to women was far too often their partners or ex-partners. His deadbeat of a father terrorized Andy's mother right up until Andy's growth spurt aged fourteen. Taller than the man he'd spent his childhood afraid of, he'd intervened that last time his dad had threatened his mom. Channeling years of fear and rage he'd somehow had the strength to throw the man against the kitchen wall, and then he'd stood above him with a knife his dad had known he was absolutely capable of using. *Never come back,* he'd said. He hadn't.

So yeah, he was checking out Violet's ex's apartment first.

The cab hadn't quite stopped moving as Andy threw easily twice the fare onto the passenger seat as he leapt onto 52nd Street outside Matt McGoldrick's red-brick apartment building.

He jogged to the entry, pushed through the revolving glass door, and caught the gaze of the doorman manning the concierge desk to the side of the lobby.

His cellphone vibrated in the back pocket of his jeans, and he paused as he yanked it out. It was Shadow Ops. He pressed the phone hard against his ear.

"We've found something," the intelligence officer said without preamble. "Remember that laptop found in the cabin where Ms Chapman was held hostage? It's owned by a shell company that's owned by another shell company and so on."

"I'll need you to get to the point."

"Of course," the woman said briskly. "And the point is we've been able to link *one* of those companies to a Matt McGoldrick. Ms Chapman's ex-boyfriend. He's a self-employed software developer, and that's about all we've got on him so far."

"I've just arrived at the fuckers building."

"Great. Hold there. Give us another fifteen minutes and we'll have access to the security vision and swipe card access. The team here is trying to determine McGoldrick's location and movements today. With any luck we'll sight Ms Chapman. Backup is also being organized as we speak, although we'll need to know more before we can issue your instructions." There was a brief pause. "Torres? Can you confirm you understand the requirement to wait for instruction?"

Andy ended the call as he strode towards the

concierge desk. No way was he patiently waiting while Violet was in danger. If she was in this building, the doorman would know. He wasn't fucking around waiting for security vision.

But the silver-haired doorman spoke before he could.

"Mr McGoldrick told me to buzz you straight through," the man said in a clipped accent. He frowned. "But I thought there were two of you?"

Thinking fast, Andy replied easily. "There are. I'm early." He gave a dry laugh. "Out of curiosity, how did you know I was here to see Matt?"

Did McGoldrick know he was here? How? His involvement in Violet's rescue had been totally erased from official police records.

The concierge looked sheepish. "Mr McGoldrick was typically direct in his request: 'Buzz through the two big dudes with tatts as soon as they arrive.'"

So McGoldrick wasn't expecting Andy, specifically. But he was expecting two large men. *Why?* That couldn't be good.

"Matt told me his ex might be here," Andy said casually. "Violet? Has she arrived?"

"Yes," the man replied carefully.

Andy laughed, even as trepidation pooled in his gut. "She's a cool chick," he said. "Can you buzz me through?"

He needed to be at that apartment *now*.

The doorman nodded. "She *is* a cool chick," he said, in a tone unlike the formal politeness of before. "I believe she was only here to collect some of her belongings," he added pointedly. "I expect her to leave *shortly.*"

"She will," Andy said. She would. If he had his way she'd be in his arms and out of this damn building within minutes. He strode towards the brass doors of the elevator as the doorman picked up the intercom handset to notify McGoldrick of Andy's arrival.

"What did you say your name was?" the doorman called out moments before the elevator doors swished shut.

Andy didn't answer. Instead, he pushed the button for Level 12, and broke into a run the moment the lift completed its journey.

Almost there, Violet.

MATT MADE Violet shuffle and jump her way from the bedroom to the study, where he manhandled her into the swivel desk chair. He placed her glasses back on with exaggerated care that made her recoil.

His gaze narrowed. "We were good once," he mused.

Violet swallowed the urge to argue with him. Looking at him now, she realized their entire relationship was a microcosm of her youth – Matt embodied the self-important, judgmental people who'd scorned her, and who she'd once been desperate to prove wrong with her success. Their relationship had been toxic from the start.

But what would arguing achieve?

Matt's gaze darted to the front door several times. Was he expecting someone?

The familiar buzz of the intercom answered her question.

She tried to think as Matt left the study to respond. She wasn't tied to the chair, and the silk ties around her wrists were more forgiving than the zip ties used by the brute and the boss. She wriggled her wrists to loosen their hold as Matt cut off the dulcet tones of the doorman, then strode to open the front door for whoever he was expecting.

Violet doubted anyone Matt would let into his apartment while she was tied up in clear view in his study was going to be of any help to her. The opposite was far more likely, given she now knew Matt's willingness to delegate violence to others.

Her heart beat against her ribs as she desperately tried to tug her hands and ankles free. But the ties, while looser, held firm.

From where she sat she could see into the living space, but not up the short hall that led to the front door. She scanned the study for a potential weapon as she fought frustration and helplessness, her gaze landing on a crystal diamond-shaped paperweight she'd won at a Curtis Pharmaceutical Awards Gala.

She could not *let Matt destroy her again.*

"Who the fuck—" she heard Matt exclaim - followed by a gasp, then a thud and a groan.

"Violet!"

It couldn't be.

Andy. Andy. *How?*

"Here!" she called out, shoving herself to her feet

awkwardly as she staggered towards the study door in utter disbelief.

And there Andy was in the middle of Matt's apartment, his size making the small space even smaller, his eyes dark and his face lined with exhaustion.

Matt lay crumpled and discarded against the wall.

The tie at her ankles gave way, and then she was running towards Andy.

"How?" she managed, before Andy threw his arms around her, dragging her close.

He was so warm, so strong. *So safe.*

Tears stung her eyes.

"How did you find me?" she whispered as he pressed a kiss to the top of her hair.

"Later," he said, taking a step back and spinning her around so he could untie her wrists in a handful of efficient movements. Then he spun her back to face him. He leaned close. "We need to get out of here," he said seriously. "Someone is coming."

She nodded. Yes, whoever Matt had really been expecting.

She glanced at her ex-boyfriend as he began to stir.

"Let's go," she said.

Andy grasped her hand and tugged her down the hall. At the front door he looked through the peep-hole.

"We're clear," he murmured. He glanced at her. "We'll take the stairs, try to avoid McGoldrick's heavies on their way up."

She nodded. He twisted the door handle and pushed

it open slightly, again glancing down the hall before pulling her out after him.

She took a deep breath as the door clicked shut. *They were going to be okay.*

But a handful of steps down the hall, the elevator dinged. They broke into a run, Violet glancing over her shoulders as they ran for the stairs.

Please just be one of Matt's neighbors.

But it wasn't. Instead, it was two men cut from the same cloth as the brute and the boss.

"That's her," one barked.

And a moment later there was a sound she'd never heard before – a dull crack. And suddenly she was falling, tripped up by something on the ground in front of her.

By *Andy.*

He no longer held her hand, and as she tumbled to the carpet she saw the tear in the knit of his grey sweater as she landed beside him.

He'd been shot.

But before she could scream, a rough hand covered her lips while another dragged her away.

TWENTY-ONE

"You didn't get any fucking blood on the carpet outside, did you?" Violet's ex demanded as his thugs dragged him through the apartment.

The bullet had only glanced Andy's shoulder. Hurt like hell, but he'd be okay. Still, he made his body a deadweight as he was dragged by his armpits, feigning shock or a loss of consciousness. These guys were amateurs, he had no doubt. Dudes thought they were tough, but they weren't trained. Their only advantage was their firearms.

Not an insignificant advantage, to be fair. He'd be armed himself if he'd been prepared to wait for a later flight to allow time to stow a firearm in checked baggage. Or if he'd waited for the backup Shadow Ops had promised.

But both options would've meant he wouldn't be here right now. Unarmed or not, at least he was here to protect Violet. And fuck... he'd do anything to protect her.

"No," the taller of the two thugs said. "Glock's got a silencer. No one's going to know."

Andy gritted his teeth as he was dropped carelessly against the floorboards.

McGoldrick grunted. He sat behind his desk with his fingers steepled together like a goddamn lord of the manor. "I've been clear several times. I don't want any mess anywhere near me." He shook his head. "How hard is that to understand?"

"You wanted the dude and the chick to get away?" the tall thug asked.

"You want to get your bonus?" Matt asked in a low monotone.

Andy kept his eyelids at half mast, his gaze on the dull metal of each thug's firearms. The tall one had his pointed casually in his direction. The other gun was far too close to Violet, who'd been tossed onto a small brown leather armchair in the corner of the room.

Matt winced as he got to his feet – not surprising as Andy had thrown him against the wall with all his strength the moment the asshole had opened his apartment door. Despite Andy's situation, it was satisfying to see the fucker in pain – even if he deserved far worse for what he'd done to Violet.

"Who the fuck are you?" Matt asked.

He was unsurprised by the kick delivered to his gut before he had a chance to reply.

"No!" Violet cried.

Matt kicked him again as Violet came to her feet. A

hand on her shoulder shoved her back down as Andy spat out a reply.

"Andy Torres."

McGoldrick chuckled. "Ah. The barista with the muscles my men threw in the Colorado river." His gaze was dismissive as it raked over his body, prone on the floor. "You should've just drowned, dude. You have no idea who you're dealing with here. You thought a few rounds in a boxing ring meant you could play hero?" He laughed as he shook his head.

Andy didn't respond, but this was good. Andy's military career wasn't secret, but a google search of his name certainly didn't reveal it – let alone that he'd been special forces. Too much further investigation by anyone would be picked up by Shadow Operations' online monitoring. His history could be found if you tried hard enough, but if you did – Shadow Ops would know.

McGoldrick clearly hadn't gone beneath the surface. McGoldrick was the man who didn't know who he was dealing with here. Neither did his heavies.

Was it an advantage that cancelled out his lack of a weapon?

It would have to be.

Violet sat perfectly still on the armchair she'd once curled up on while she'd read for hours. Right now, she was stiff as a board, the facsimile of the brute standing close by, his gun pointed at her temple.

Was Andy okay?

He'd barely moved after that last kick from Matt, but his bullet wound appeared to have stopped bleeding at least, the stain on his shoulder growing no larger. She focused on the rhythmic rise and fall of his ribs, trying to slow her own panicked breathing to align with his.

The other brute stood over him, gun aimed at Andy's chest.

"Should we take 'em now, then?" that brute asked Matt. "The usual place?"

The usual place? How many people had Matt made disappear? As it was absolutely clear that was what these men were here for.

"Soon," Matt replied. He turned to face her. "I need to finish things up with Violet here, first."

His lips stretched across his teeth in somewhat of a smile.

How the hell was I ever attracted to this man?

He was utterly foul in every possible way.

Matt swept past her to tug the desk chair forward until it was maybe a foot from her sneakers. Then he grabbed the closed silver laptop on his desk before plonking himself in front of her. He was so close his knees bumped hers, and she flinched.

He laughed. "You used to be gagging for me to touch you," he said. "Honestly, if there was any other option, I would've done things differently." He shrugged. "But hey, tens of millions of dollars makes up for missing out on your sweet ass." He flicked his gaze at Andy, who still hadn't moved. "You let that dumbass fuck you?" He shuddered. "Thought you had more class than that. Guess that's your white trash heritage, huh?"

Violet arranged her mouth into a perfectly straight line, swallowing the curses she wished she could unleash. Her gaze dropped to Andy, who still hadn't moved.

For an infinitesimal moment his gaze caught hers, before his lids drifted part way closed again. But that gaze was sharp. Not glazed with pain. Not semi-conscious.

He has a plan.

Of course he did. He'd tracked her across Colorado. He'd saved her from her kidnappers. He'd somehow followed her to New York. He wasn't going to give up now.

He wasn't going to give up on her now.

Now wasn't the time to comprehend what that meant, or how it felt. But it did straighten her spine and silence any urge to react to Matt's bullshit.

"Still think I'm jealous, Violet?" he shuffled in his seat as he dug into the front pocket of his jeans, before theatrically tugging the flash drive out and thrusting it in the air. "Still think you're so much cleverer than me?"

She held his gaze but remained silent.

"No words, huh?" He shook his head. "What were you trying to do, Vi?" He rotated the flash drive in his fingers as he looked at it. "Let me guess, this is a copy of the data that *almost* tripped me up. Did me a favor, really, what you discovered. Found my only error, and there won't be another one, trust me." He gripped the flash drive so hard his knuckles turned white. "What was your plan? Take this to the cops?" He laughed. "*No one* would believe you, even with this so-called evidence. Why would they even listen? You're trash, Violet. Tried so hard to be something you weren't, fooling everyone you could have this New York life, even me."

"What are you talking about?" Violet said, unable to stop herself. "*You* ruined my life, not me."

"But no one believed you," he said, his chuckle low and smug. "You didn't. You know what you are. And the cops will know, too. They won't listen."

"Yes, they would," Violet said firmly, knowing it was true. "I'm not the woman I was back then. I can't be manipulated into believing I'm less than anyone else. Less than you."

Matt threw back his head as he laughed. "Fuck's sake Violet, you have a gun pointed at your head and you're believing that shit? *You are trash.*" He swiveled in his chair to face Andy. "This guy make you believe you're not?" He shook his head. "Man, he must have really wanted to get in your pants."

But even as Matt tried to tear her down, it was only *his* insecurities that were on show. His cruel words did nothing to her as she knew what they were: lies. They always had been.

Just like in the walk-in closet where she'd had the revelation that at some point in the last twelve months she'd chosen Falcon as her home, and not a stopping point, she realized now that she believed – for the first time in her life – that she was enough. She was worthy of acceptance, of care and of protection. Every person waiting on her porch when she'd arrived home from

Guneo yesterday morning had taught her that with their presence.

And the man on the floor with a bullet hole in his shoulder, who twice now raced headlong into danger to save her... what had he taught her?

That I'm worthy of love.

Andy hadn't said the words – and maybe she was wrong and he didn't love her at all – but... she loved him.

She loved him so much. Only in this moment did she grasp the reality of her love for Andy Torres, but it had been there, beneath the surface, for a very long time. Maybe right from the beginning, when he'd so staunchly defended her from her old English Teacher, when no one had *ever* defended her before.

The way Andy made her feel... that sense of irresistible connection and the impossibility of wanting anyone else. The way his need for her was overwhelming, and his urge to protect her was without boundary. *That* was what she deserved. That was what she was worthy of.

That type of love.

"No smart reply this time from the brilliant Violet Chapman?" Matt followed her gaze. "Oh, I see. How sweet. I can see you're keen to use the limited time you have left staring at your dumbass wannabe hero, but I need to interrupt you for a moment. I want to show you *exactly* how clever I am." Another smug chuckle. "You know, I almost took you up on the offer to show me this data that night we had dinner in the NoMad district, just so I could tell you it was *me*. But, well... I knew you didn't have the fortitude, or the genius, to support what I'd done. But I can at least walk you through it now."

Matt flipped open the silver laptop, then bent forward as he inserted the USB connector into the port.

As Matt focused on the laptop, so too did the two brutes. The man closest to Violet leaned forward to peer in curiosity at the laptop screen, his firearm dropping slightly to aim at the carpet instead of her. And the tall man who'd loomed over Andy, he'd relaxed his pose. Yes, the gun still pointed at Andy, but the man's attention was also on the laptop, his weight propped on one leg casually.

Matt had opened up the flash drive's file folder, tapping firmly on the trackpad as he scrolled through its contents.

She met Andy's gaze. His eyes were now open and direct. She followed his gaze as it darted to the man above him, then to the gunman beside her, then to Matt.

Wait, he mouthed.

She frowned. He'd just told her to wait before she did... what? They'd only get one chance, and she was no Delta Force operator.

He mouthed a word she didn't understand. Then he mouthed it again.

Logic.

Of course. Back at the cabin he'd asked her how she'd known what to do to give him the shot at The Boss. *Logic*, she'd said. But really it'd been instinctive, the deadly blade near her skin sending her logical brain into over-drive. Again her life was in danger, but this time she had precious moments to think... but the logical outcome was the same. She knew what to do: *give Andy a chance to save them.*

"Where the fuck is it, Violet?" Matt said abruptly, his fingers tapping urgently on the laptop's trackpad. "How many goddamn photos did you take of some college toga party from 2013?"

Had Matt realized yet?

"Try the folder labelled Graduation," she said helpfully.

"Why on earth would *you* save a Curtis Pharmaceutical analytics dashboard in a folder labelled Graduation?"

Why would Violet Chapman save classified corporate data on a ten-year-old flash drive full of college pics?

The obvious answer was – she hadn't. She'd saved it to a hardware encrypted flash drive in line with Curtis Pharmaceutical's policies for the transportation of private data. She *always* followed procedure.

All Matt had was a flash drive full of her UChicago memories.

She held Andy's gaze again. He knew nothing about why Matt had kidnapped her, or the dashboards, or the flash drive she'd come here to find. But had he worked out that Matt was about to go batshit crazy?

Now, he mouthed.

"It's not here. *Where is it* you stupid bitch, what did you come here for if—"

With her knees near touching Matt's, it was easy for Violet to grab the laptop and throw it as hard as she could at the gunman by her side. In the same movement she launched herself at Matt, sending the swivel chair careening towards the window as a muffled gunshot rang out behind her and Matt shouted in her ear.

"Andy!" she screamed, as the chair containing her and Matt hit the wall with a crash and they both fell to the floor behind the desk. She clambered to her knees, kicking free of Matt's hands as he tried to grab at her while he shouted abuse.

"*Kill them*," he shouted. "End this *now*."

"Get *down*, Violet," Andy ordered, as she came to her feet and glimpsed him in the process of slamming the shorter brute against the wall, his big hand wrapped around the man's wrist as they both fought for control of the weapon. As another shot rang out and Violet dropped back down behind the desk.

Where was the other brute? What if he shot Andy?

She peered beneath the desk to see the shape of the taller man laying almost exactly where Andy had been, the man's handgun several feet from his unconscious grasp.

Violet had no idea what special forces move had allowed Andy to render a man comatose in seconds, but clearly he hadn't been able to grab the Glock before launching himself at the second brute. She began crawling under the desk towards it as the sounds of Andy wrestling with the brute continued.

"Where do you think you're going Vi?" said Matt, grabbing her ankles. This time she didn't have the advantage of surprise and momentum, and his grip held firm.

"Let go!" she hissed, as Matt tried to drag her back towards him. She kicked and struggled, but while he didn't succeed in pulling her back, he'd halted her progress forward.

There was a crunching noise and the sounds of wrestling abruptly ended, followed by the thump of a body against the floor.

"Andy!" she screamed, unable to see who had fallen from beneath the desk with the drawers blocking her view of that side of the room.

Suddenly Matt let her go and she crawled forward frantically.

"Andy!" she screamed again as she emerged from the other side of the desk.

And he was there. Right there, offering her his hand.

"Oh, Andy—" but her relief was interrupted by a glancing blow to her head. "Owww!" she gasped, in surprise, twisting as she realized Matt had followed her beneath the desk, something in his hand. His eyes were hard.

He lifted the object in his hand again. It was the crystal paperweight. Heavy and pointed at the tip. A tip that was dark with...*her blood?*

She reached a hand to her temple, shocked to feel wet stickiness beneath her fingers. Desperately she tried to escape from the close confines of the desk as Matt raised the paper weight again.

"No, Matt, don't—"

But then the paperweight fell harmlessly to the floor as Andy's much larger hand grabbed Matt's wrist in midair and yanked him effortlessly out from beneath the desk.

A moment later Matt was face down on the floor, Andy's knee in his back.

Violet climbed shakily to her feet, shock and relief making her woozy. She gripped the edge of the desk as she surveyed the room and the three felled men scattered across the study's floor.

Matt lifted his head to look at her. "You still don't have any proof," he spat.

Andy twisted Matt's arm tighter behind his back, and the smaller man gasped.

"Man, I don't know what proof you're talking about, but I reckon the decades you're getting for soliciting felony kidnapping means you won't ever be bothering Violet again."

Impossibly, Matt laughed. "You think I'll stop building my empire in prison? It'll be waiting for me when I get out."

Andy shoved his knee harder against Matt's back. "Shut up, dickhead," he said.

But Matt didn't. "You haven't won, Violet."

"It was never a competition," she replied.

"Are you able to grab that firearm, please?" Andy asked, nodding at the Glock still on the floor. "And something to tie this asshole's wrists?"

She crossed the small room as Matt kept on talking.

"Of course it was. You were constantly trying to one-up me."

Violet wrapped her fingers around the handle of the

Glock. It felt foreign and uncomfortable, but she was incredibly grateful *she* held it, and not Matt or one of his army of thugs. Because of Andy – again – she was safe.

"No, I wasn't," she said firmly. "I was trying to impress you, always. Feel worthy of you." She shook her head. "What a waste of time that was."

"Exactly," Matt agreed. "You were *never* worthy of me."

Matt cried out as Andy twisted his arm even tighter – but Violet just laughed.

"You're never going to make me feel small again, Matt," she said. "I'm not the woman I was, and I won't allow your pathetic insecurities to drag me down."

Matt spluttered. "I've *won*, Violet, no matter what lies you tell yourself or because of some lucky kung fu move your barista learned on YouTube."

Andy rolled his eyes. "If you want me to shut him up for a while, just say the word."

"No, I've got it," she said. She jogged to where Andy had discarded the ties that had once bound her wrists out in the living area. She grabbed them both, and moments later Matt was secured while Andy unlaced the brutes' boots to tie their wrists and ankles. Not one of the bad guys was going anywhere.

Then she stood over Matt where he lay helpless but defiant, despite the gun she held tight in her right hand.

Andy tugged his phone out of his back pocket and made a call. Moments later he spoke. "Cops were already on their way; they won't be long."

So many questions swirled in Violet's brain – but

they could wait. "Are you okay?" she asked, staring at his shoulder.

He shrugged. "It was nothing. Barely a flesh wound. You?"

She touched her hairline, but the graze near her temple had long stopped bleeding. "I'm totally fine," she said. She met Andy's gaze. "Thanks to you. Again. *Thank you.*"

He ran a hand through his hair. "I'd prefer this to be the last time you scare me to death, Violet."

She nodded, her lips quirking. "Agreed."

He shook his head. "Fuck, Vi, if I'd lost you..." His gaze travelled to the smashed laptop near the feet of one of the brutes. "Is that what you came to New York for? This evidence that asshole keeps talking about? And your kidnapping was linked to that?"

"Yeah," she said. She gestured at Matt. "He thought I knew about this elaborate cybercrime he has going, and had me kidnapped to warn me off it. But he told me all that shit that went down here in New York – that destroyed my life – was his doing. I guess you heard the rumors?"

Andy shrugged. "Not in detail. Always figured it was all bullshit."

"Thank you," she said quietly. "I wish others had felt that way. I wish *I* had." She shook her head. "All of this – the kidnapping, this evidence, it's all related to software Matt wrote to steal millions of dollars without anyone noticing – but I'd noticed, even if I hadn't realized it yet." She stared down at the gun in her hand. Her finger wasn't on the trigger, but the gun still felt ugly and dangerous in her palm. "He threatened me – well, threatened my Nanna, Casey, and *you*, too, Andy, if I spoke, or even worked in the analytics field again. And I couldn't have that, I couldn't have this pathetic man control me like that."

"So you flew to New York."

"I had to. Matt's undermined me before. He's twisted everything to change the narrative and his hacking skills would mean nothing would ever be tracked back to him. I knew if all I had was words Matt would never be arrested, and speaking would've done nothing but put the people I care about at risk. I needed evidence."

"You won't find it," Matt said, but his insolent tone was waning.

"Dude, honestly?" Andy asked. "You're done. Shut the fuck up."

There was the soft clunk of the apartment's front door being unlocked. The police had arrived.

She stepped closer to Matt and he rolled his eyes. But it was all bravado. As the police called out to Andy and footsteps entered the tiny apartment, Matt had gone pale.

If he wasn't literally the person she hated most in the world, she would almost feel sorry for him.

Instead, she dropped down onto her haunches and looked him in the eye.

"It wasn't a competition, Matt," she said firmly, and she held up a hand when he went to argue. "But as it's clearly important to you, I want to make something clear. *I won.* I am better, stronger, happier... *everything* more than when I left New York. I thought you destroyed my life, but from that rubble I've created a life I wouldn't change for the world."

Matt snorted. "That's meaningless sentimental garbage—"

She beamed a smile at him. "Fine!" she said, as she stood up. "This should mean something to you, then." She reached into the front pocket of her jeans and tugged out an object she turned casually over in her fingers. It was the encrypted flash drive she'd found exactly where she'd left it – in the pocket of her favorite coat - as she'd scrambled to her feet when Matt had surprised her in his closet.

Matt looked like he was going to vomit.

She grinned as she looked to Andy.

"Reckon we've got a clearcut winner here, wouldn't you say McGoldrick?" Andy asked, with that same sparkle in his gaze from the day they'd met.

But Matt didn't answer.

Minutes later they were out of the apartment and into the elevator, a detective by their side. Exhaustion and shock threatened to overwhelm her – but then Andy gripped her fingers. She looked up to meet his gaze as the brass elevator doors swished open in the building's foyer.

"Andy—" she began, unsure if she was going to ask him a million questions or declare her newly realized love, her brain foggy with relief and pure joy to be safe and at Andy's side.

"Goddamn, Torres, you reckon you could leave us something to do?" asked a familiar voice.

Violet frowned as Andy tugged her out of the elevator and in front of Caleb Grey, Sam Taberner and Dev McCarthy.

"Twice now you've stolen our thunder," continued Caleb, shaking his head. "It's greedy, I tell you." He caught Violet's gaze. "Don't you think, Vi?"

Her gaze drifted from Caleb, to Sam, to Dev – then back to Andy. She was utterly confused.

"Andy?" she asked. "I feel like I'm missing something. Why is everyone from Cars & Coffee in New York?"

He smiled and squeezed her hand gently. "Violet," he said. "I'd like you to meet the Shadow Team."

TWENTY-TWO

It was hours later, and Violet had just finished giving her statement to a pair of detectives at NYPD's Midtown North Precinct. She walked into the foyer to four men waiting for her.

The Shadow Team.

Violet had to admit, it was a cool name.

However, that was about all she knew, with Andy's brief explanation seriously light on detail: *we do covert assignments that use our special forces skills when the police or military can't help.*

But the detectives had whisked her away, so until now her many questions had remained unasked.

Andy jumped to his feet the moment he saw her. "Violet—" he said, striding towards her. And then she was in his arms, his strong arms holding her tight. For the first time in days, she felt her body truly relax as she sunk into his strength and warmth. Her questions – about the Shadow Team and more importantly about *this* – about *them* – were forgotten in the magic of Andy Torres' embrace.

"Let's keep this reunion snappy." Dev's words were gruff. "Wolf's organized for his private jet to get us back to Falcon, and I've had about enough of New York."

"You've had about enough of Falcon, too," Andy pointed out, lifting his face from Violet's hair. She turned in his arms to see the other three men had all stood, ready to leave.

"He's had enough of most everywhere, I'd suggest," added Caleb. "Dev's foul mood is location agnostic."

Dev's lips quirked in an almost grin.

"You smiled!" Violet exclaimed.

But instantly any evidence of levity disappeared.

"And we're back to Dev's regularly scheduled programing," Caleb laughed, shaking his head.

"We out of here?" Sam asked.

Andy grinned. "Let's go."

"Who's Wolf?" Violet asked as the 12-seater private jet reached its cruising altitude high above New York.

"He owns Shadow Operations," Andy replied, unclipping his seatbelt and relaxing into his light tan leather seat. Violet sat beside him, with the rest of the Shadow Team behind them in a group of seats facing each other across a glossy timber table. They were light-heartedly arguing over which of the dozens of card games Wolf kept on the jet they'd play.

"I'm not playing Monopoly Deal *again*," Dev

complained from behind them. "I don't know which dickhead agreed to play that stupid game all the way to Germany that time, but I'm done. My Monopoly quota has been exceeded."

"*You* were that dickhead," Caleb said smugly, "when you wagered against me in Spades."

"Dev is a dickhead," Tabs agreed. "But this is a democratic society. We're having a vote. All in favor of Uno?"

Dev and Tabs immediately *aye-ed* in agreement.

"Andy, man, need your help back here—" Caleb began.

Andy twisted in his chair to look over the headrest. "Reckon you can let me prioritize Violet over your squabbling?"

A grumbling sound of agreement officially left him and Violet - for the first time since they'd fallen asleep together in Violet's bed - somewhat alone.

"Was that flight to Germany a Shadow Team thing?" Violet asked quietly, drawing her knees up so she was curled up on her seat.

"Yeah. A rare job where we all went."

"What was it for?" she asked.

He shrugged. "Can't tell you that, sorry."

They'd successfully extracted the kidnapped five-year-old son of a mining magnate from a mountain lodge just outside of Frankfurt.

"But you *can* tell me the Shadow Team exists?" She frowned.

"Tabs would've decided that with Wolf. But I agree, after today you were going to be asking questions."

"Like how you knew I flew to New York."

"Exactly. I had help finding you in that cabin outside Guneo, too."

She nodded. "I'm a little annoyed I didn't work this out sooner. I work with you guys every day. I should've picked up on some super-secret spy side hustle."

He grinned. "If you had, Wolf would've asked us some tough questions. Keeping the team secret is kinda important."

"Who *is* Wolf, though? What kind of guy creates a team like this?"

"A rich one," Andy said simply. Then added, "to be fair, I don't know anything about the guy. Tabs is his main contact, he's the one who assigns our jobs and manages our schedule."

"That's why Sam manages your work roster! To juggle it with Shadow Team work?"

"Yup. He's pretty good at it, although doesn't much care about the Cars & Coffee roster. He cares more about special ops than oil filters, sorry."

Her eyebrows drew together. "So, Cars & Coffee is like a front for the Shadow Team?"

"Yep. It was Sam's idea, and it's brilliant, really. Without it we'd get way more scrutiny. Plus, it's a great place for the armory."

"The *armory*?" she exclaimed.

He grinned. He was enjoying telling her all of this. "Secret door behind the break room."

She shook her head. "Wow. And you work with law enforcement agencies and the military?"

He shrugged. "A lot of private individuals, too. Sometimes for the wealthy who can afford to use us, and sometimes pro bono. Like Cherry."

"Wow. Again." Violet hugged her knees tighter. Then sat up straight. "Wait – was she really engaged to Sam before she arrived in Falcon?"

"Nope. Long story, but...nope."

"And she knows about the Shadow Team?"

"Yes. But she's the only person in Falcon who does, other than you."

A cabin crew member approached to offer them drinks.

"That's a lot of trust you've put in me."

He shrugged. "It's you, Violet. I'm not worried. And clearly neither is Shadow Operations."

She smiled, her gaze dropping to the bottle of water she held in her hand. "What happens...tomorrow, I guess? Back at Cars and Coffee?"

Before Andy could answer, another voice called out.

"I don't want you back at work until Wednesday at the earliest, Violet," said Tabs. He stood and rested his hands on the top of his seat as he looked down at them. "You were kidnapped. Take the whole week, actually. Decompress. Sleep." He shrugged. "Whatever." He caught Andy's gaze. "You too, Torres. Figure you might need time to..." His words drifted off as he looked to Violet, then back to Andy, then back to Violet again. He cleared his throat. "Figured you might need some time," he said firmly.

Sam sat down.

Then almost instantly stood up again. "Oh, and Violet, when you *do* come back to work, you can either keep on doing what you've been doing, or you can help The Shadow Team. And Shadow Ops too, if you want. Wolf has heard of you, and is *very* impressed by your data analytics career. He's keen to talk if you're interested, and negotiate a salary in line with your New York expectations."

Violet blinked at Sam a few times. "This is all a little overwhelming."

"It's all up to you," Tabs continued. "Although I'd *really* like you to take over our scheduling. Andy might think I'm pretty good at it, but I hate it."

"Eavesdropping, Tabs?" Andy asked.

He shrugged unapologetically. "I'd suggest you wait until we're home before you make your grand apology to Violet."

"What apology?" she asked, her gaze darting over to Andy.

Tabs grinned. "Lucky guess," he said. His lips quirked. "Based on knowing Torres is an idiot."

He slapped Andy on the shoulder than sank back into his seat and out of view.

It was late when Violet arrived home with Andy.

This time there was no Falcon welcoming party – as this time her adventures would not be shared with the town, as directed by Shadow Ops - but there was a basket at her front door from Casey, with a note.

. . .

THE PUMPKIN PIE IS EXCELLENT, as my mom made it. The lasagna may be excellent or appalling, I had an awful thought as I drove here that maybe I got the salt and sugar measurements backwards? Anyway, if I did, I've told Minh at Pho Sure to charge your meal to my tab – which isn't a thing that actually exists but Minh told me she will hunt me down at the library if I don't pay, so you're good. Casey xx.

HER EYES STUNG, and she gave a tight smile as she looked up at Andy.

"You okay?" he asked, Casey's basket in his arms as she fumbled for her front door key.

"Yeah," she said, the word just a little wobbly. She pushed the door open, leading Andy inside and into the kitchen. "I guess... what I told Matt, it was the truth. About not changing my life since New York for the world." She shook her head. "I guess that's why I haven't finished any of the big city job applications I've started." She leaned against the countertop as she looked at Andy. "I'm happy here. Back in Falcon, the place I once hated, and I thought hated me."

"How could anyone hate you?"

She laughed. "I know, right?" But she shook her head. "But I guess from all of this, what I've learned is the good people that cared about me were always there, even back then. My Nanna, Casey, and more, even – like I'm on the

Rodeo Committee with my old calculus teacher, who I'd somehow forgotten was quietly encouraging when I turned things around in my senior year. There were lots of judgmental assholes too, but not everyone. And now I've stopped being obsessed with proving myself worthy to *everyone*, like Matt said, I've realized I already deserved – and had - the respect of the people that matter."

"Yes, you do," Andy said.

She nodded. "I also know I should've told you I was going to New York," she said. "I knew it then, too, but a lifetime of independence – both through choice and otherwise – made it difficult. Like I said, your protection of me sat uneasily. People don't *care* for Violet Chapman. They reject me. And I thought your rejection of me was inevitable."

"For good reason," he said. "I'm the world's biggest asshole for rejecting you twice."

"Three times," she said. "I totally count you ghosting me when the cops arrived at the cabin."

Andy winced. "Three times," he conceded. "I'm so sorry, Violet—"

She held up a hand. "You also saved my life twice, Andy, risking your own in the process. From what I overheard from the Shadow Team, you didn't follow procedure, you didn't wait for backup in your desperation to save me." She grinned. "Doesn't quite cancel it out, but it's a start."

His smile was rueful.

"*That's* what I want, Andy," she said. "I want that..."

she swallowed, not quite ready to say the word. "... passion. Hopefully without the need to fight for my life in the future, but definitely that overwhelming... need. That connection."

"*Mine*," Andy said, then his eyes widened. "Sorry, I just—"

Again she interrupted. "No. Don't apologize. Don't make how we feel for each other something toxic and awful, when to me it's anything but." She shook her head. "If you're going to do that, let's end this conversation now. Let's end *this* now."

She took a deep breath as her heart squeezed with pain. She'd known this would happen. She'd known it, deep, deep inside.

He stepped closer and took her hand. "I wasn't apologizing for that," he said firmly. "I was apologizing for interrupting."

She frowned. "You weren't? But what about all you said about your dad? About what's happened since the siege?"

He lifted his chin as he studied her. "You're expecting me to reject you again," he said. "You're telling me all this, trusting me with all this, but you're waiting for me to walk away."

She nodded. "I know now what I deserve," she said. "I know what I want. But I can't let you hurt me again, Andy."

He squeezed her hand tight. "I will *never* forgive myself for contributing to the doubt you're feeling right now, Violet. *Ever*."

Her lips quirked. "It's okay. I can't make you feel the way I want you to feel."

"And how's that?" he asked urgently. "What feeling do you doubt I have for you?"

She tugged her hand free. "That's cruel," she said. "To make me say it."

He ran both his hands through his hair as he met her gaze. "It's love, isn't it, Violet?" he said, like he was stunned that was what she was thinking. "Violet, *never* doubt that I love you," he said fiercely. "Never, *ever*, doubt that."

"Pardon me?" she said, reaching to grab onto the countertop as her knees went weak. "Did you just say—"

"Of course I did," he said. "I love you, Violet. I can't even say when it began, but it's been months. A year – who knows? I was in the thick of loving you with no clue because I'm exactly the fucking idiot that Tabs called me."

She sucked in a breath. "You *are* my Mr Darcy," she said.

"What?"

She gave a huff of laughter. "I'll explain later."

It was what Darcy said to Elizabeth about his love for her in the final chapters of Pride and Prejudice: *I was in the middle before I knew that I had begun.* She couldn't quite believe this, that her thoughts two nights earlier, when she'd returned home to the BBC drama blaring in her lounge room and so foolishly cast herself as Lizzie Bennett and Andy as Darcy could play out to not be foolish at all...

No. Wait. She had to be sensible here. His words of love resolved nothing.

"But Andy," she said. "What about what you told me last night? I don't believe for a moment you're the violent man you said you are. But you used that as a reason to push me away, and you would've used it again if I hadn't run away to New York. What's changed?"

She couldn't have Andy's twisted self-belief be as damaging as her own had been.

He shoved his hands into the front pockets of his jeans. "I made a phone call," he said gruffly, "while you were giving your statement at the precinct." His gaze darted towards the window as he shifted his weight uncomfortably. "Last night, you asked me if Natalie had felt in danger when I found her with Cez, and I told you no. But I didn't believe that, not really. It's what's driven my behavior these last few years, this belief that I was capable of terrorizing a woman the way my father terrorized my mom." He took a deep breath. "So, I called her, and asked." He laughed. "Sounds simple, doesn't it?" He shook his head, then held her gaze. "We didn't have a long conversation. She's married now, and her new baby was fussing in her arms. But she accepted my apology for how I reacted, and assured me she'd never, ever felt unsafe. I still know what I did wasn't okay, but the way I extrapolated that behavior to label myself as dangerous as my father... I took it too far."

Violet nodded. "Did she marry Tyler?"

"No. I called him, too. He didn't answer, but I left a message apologizing for punching him, and told him I've forgiven him for the affair with Natalie. And when I did that, I realized there was nothing to forgive. I was messed up after the Fox & Laughton, and my own behavior to distance myself from Cez and Natalie contributed to the ending of what had been the two most important relationships in my life at the time. Hearing how happy Natalie is now, I know now we never would've married, even without the Fox & Laughton or the affair. I never loved her like..." He shrugged. "Well, like I love you. But Cez – I threw that friendship away long before the affair. And now I can see that my behavior leading up to the affair, and ever since, has been about creating distance. Because living through that siege showed me the life I'd been living wasn't the life I'd wanted, but I was too scared to chase the life I *did* want, because what if that life was taken away? Now I knew that life was so fragile, could I risk the life and the love I wanted?"

She held his gaze. "Can you take that risk?"

His voice cracked. "Risking my life is so much easier than risking my heart." He swallowed. "But yes. I'd risk my life a million times for you. And a million times I'd risk my heart. I love you, Violet Chapman."

She could see the uncertainty in his gorgeous hazel eyes, and the self-doubt she was far too familiar with.

"Never doubt I love you, Andy Torres," she said, stepping close and sliding her palms from his chest to his shoulders. "Never doubt that I'm yours."

He cradled her face in his hands. "Mine," he said.

And this time the word was different. This time it

was so much more than heat, and attraction and the delicious power of possession.

This time it was raw, and real, and true.

She was his. And he was hers.

Then he kissed her and kissed her, until they were both desperate in how they tugged the clothing off each other's bodies. She was on the edge of the counter as he thrust inside her, her legs tight around his hips and words of love spilling from their lips.

He possessed her, she possessed him.

Mine. Yours. Yours. Mine.

And together they possessed each other's hearts.

EPILOGUE

ANDY LACED HIS FINGERS WITH VIOLET'S AS THEY walked into The Roost that Friday night.

They'd been practically hermits that week, splitting their time between her Nanna's place – who was now home and well now she knew Matt was behind bars – and Andy's. They'd talked, and slept and just hung out – as if trying to make up for the year they'd worked together but remained apart.

It had been wonderful. So wonderful, in fact, they were already making plans for Violet to move into Andy's place. She'd also accepted the role she'd been offered at Shadow Operations. Day to day, she'd be located at Cars & Coffee – but she'd be remotely heading up the Shadow Operations Data Analytics department. Just like Andy, Cars & Coffee would now be the front for her real career – and honestly, she couldn't be more excited to have the opportunity to use her skills to help others. It was funny how things worked out – instead of working out how to grow the profits of a pharmaceutical conglomerate, she'd be mining data to solve crimes and save lives.

She squeezed Andy's hand as she spotted the rest of the Cars & Coffee crew beside the bar, then reluctantly let him go as Cherry rushed over for a hug.

"Congratulations!" Violet exclaimed, acknowledging Cherry and Sam's engagement the night she'd been kidnapped.

"Thanks," Cherry said. Her gaze darted to Sam. "He's pretty amazing." Then she refocused on Violet. "And I'm *so* glad you and Andy have sorted your shit out, too," she said in her gentle Australian accent. "Now we just need Dev and Casey to get over themselves."

Violet raised her eyebrows. "I know what you're saying, but honestly – you really think Casey wouldn't just *be* with Dev if that's what she wanted? She isn't backwards about anything."

"True," Cherry conceded. "I guess the tension between them *could* be the same tension Dev creates between himself and literally everyone else in the universe."

Violet laughed. "Exactly."

"And Caleb there," Cherry continued, "he's enormously happy being single. So, Dev's hardly the odd one out." She paused. "Actually, Sam mentioned some other guy, Tyler Cerra? Do you know him?"

Violet nodded. "He's been working for Shadow Ops too, just independently of the Shadow Team. I don't think that's going to change anytime soon, but I know the guys have been considering it."

"Is Andy okay with it? I heard what went down."

"Yeah," Violet said. "He's the one driving it, actually. It's Tyler who isn't so sure, but Andy's patient."

Cherry laughed. "You're telling me. *How long* were you two flirting with each other? I spent one night in your vicinity and knew what was going down."

Andy had rejoined them and wrapped an arm around Violet's waist. She leaned against his warmth. "She was worth the wait," he said, looking down to catch her gaze.

"Awwwww," said Casey, joining them. "Young love is so sweet."

"Aren't we the same age—" Andy began, but he went silent as his attention focused on the entrance to The Roost.

They all followed his gaze to a woman who'd just walked in.

She had blonde hair in a messy bun and stood on her tip toes as she scanned the crowded bar.

"Do you know her?" Violet asked Andy.

He looked down at her distractedly. "No. Yes. Kind of." He shook his head. "Sorry. I need to get Caleb."

But right then, Caleb brushed past, his attention laser focused on the woman as he strode urgently towards her.

"Who is she?" Violet asked.

Andy ran a hand through his hair. "I don't know her name," he said. "But the last time I saw her was just after the first bomb exploded at the Fox and Laughton."

Stunned, Violet watched the moment the woman saw Caleb, her relief palpable across the crowded space.

And Violet didn't need to be a lipreader to work out what she said next.

I need your help, Caleb.

Please.

A moment later Caleb whisked her outside.

A NOTE FROM LEAH

Thank you for reading The Protector's Vow! Would you like to spend a little more time with Violet and Andy? I've written an extended version of the love scene at the end of Chapter 22 which is available exclusively to my newsletter subscribers. You can join my newsletter here: https://dl.bookfunnel.com/896xsxt8ax to read the chapter (you'll also get access to an exclusive novella and other bonus scenes from my books).

As I'm sure you've guessed, it's Caleb and Lucy's story that's next in the Shadow Team Six series! It will be out late in 2022/early 2023. In the meantime, make sure you've read book one The Protector's Temptation (Sam & Cherry) or check out my Elite SWAT series if you want more scorching hot, super-romantic adventure romance.

I can't wait to share more of the Shadow Team with you!

Leah xx

ABOUT THE AUTHOR

WWW.LEAH-ASHTON.COM

RITA® Award-winning author Leah Ashton writes fast-paced, sexy romantic suspense and smart, modern contemporary romance. All her books feature strong heroines, deliciously heroic heroes and swoon worthy happily ever afters.

Leah lives in Perth, Western Australia with her gorgeous husband, two amazing daughters and the best intentions to meal plan and have an effortlessly tidy home. When she's not writing, Leah loves all day breakfast, rambling conversations and laughing until she cries. She really hates cucumber. And scary movies.

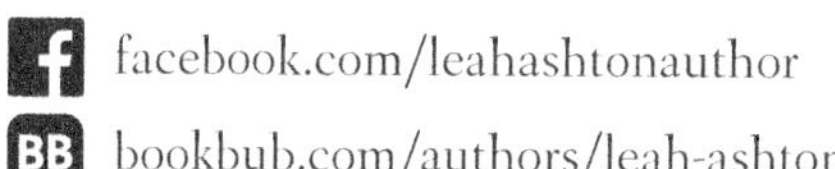

ALSO BY LEAH ASHTON

Shadow Team Six Series

The Protector's Temptation

The Protector's Vow

(Caleb, Tyler, Garrett, Dev and Wolf's stories to come!)

Elite SWAT Series

For the Fight

Out Run the Night

Danger in Trust

Beneath the Fear

Hold True

Defy the Storm

In His Sights (prequel novella)

Contemporary Romance

Secrets & Speed Dating

A Girl Less Ordinary

Why Resist a Rebel?

Beware of the Boss

Nine Month Countdown (Molyneux Sisters #1)

The Billionaire from her Past (Molyneux Sisters #2)

Behind the Billionaire's Guarded Heart (Molyneux Sisters #3)

The Prince's Fake Fiancee (Vela Ada #1)

His Pregnant Christmas Princess (Vela Ada #2)

Mining for Love (trade anthology of the Molyneux Sisters)

Made in United States
North Haven, CT
08 August 2025